For information, contact:

Gig Productions, Inc.
info@gigpros.com

ISBN 978 0 9713065 0 9

A catalogue record for this title is available from the Library of Congress.
Txu 957 – 324

Author: Mary Lauren Karlton

Layout design: Rhonda Van Buskirk

Cover design: Ilia Goshev

The Lizard of Ozzzz

A New American Allegory

by Mary Lauren Karlton

Gig Productions, Inc.
Santa Fe, NM • Santa Cruz, CA
2007

Dedicated to the many victims of

electronic privacy invasion and abuse

and to those committed to the defense

of our digital and civil liberties.

Acknowledgements

First, I would like to give a general thanks to my circle of support-ive and loving friends who have showered me with encouragement and enthusiasm during the course of this project. I would especially like to thank my technical advisor, who, paranoid at birth, chooses to remain anonymous. He has provided me with invaluable insights into the issue of digital privacy and the machinations behind tech-nologies that touch our daily lives in the cyber age. He knows who he is—a true and stalwart friend to the end. I also thank my highly competent editors, Dorothy Wall, and especially, Parthenia Hicks, a splendid writer and first-rate editor and friend. I also offer my gratitude to my cohort in creativity, Peter Sterbach, for his prodigious proofreading abilities and his thoughtful praise. Additionally, I am grateful to my readers, who assisted me with quality control and generally cheered me on, including Diana Real, Stan Goldberg. and Russell Rosenberg. I also thank cover artist Ilia Goshev, designer Rhonda Van Buskirk, and photographer Timothy Aldridge for their talent and ability to translate my vision into reality, and I thank Humberto and Mercedes Robles, who instilled in me a love of literature and the pursuit of knowledge. Finally, I offer my humble gratitude to the Muse of Creative Inspiration and Imagination for allowing me to play in her magical, mysterious realm.

Prologue

"But the wicked witch isn't dead yet, Mommy!" wailed Kirsten. "We can't do anything until she's dead!"

"Girls, will you get off that computer and listen to me! Your dinner's stone cold and you're three weeks behind in your homework. If you're not down here in five minutes, I'm coming up to get you!"

Charlotte Meyerstone clicked the off button on the intercom in her kitchen. She took ten puffs from her cigarette and smashed the butt into the stainless steel sink before storming up the thickly carpeted stairs to the playroom.

Kirsten and her younger sister, Amanda, were huddled together over the computer. Kirsten shoved the mouse into Amanda's hand. "Here, Amanda, you kill her before Mom gets here."

Amanda grabbed the mouse, frantically maneuvering the pointer all over the computer screen. "Kirsten, I can't, she's moving too fast. Look, she's laughing at us. And those flying blue monkeys keep getting in the way. I can't. I can't kill her!" Tears of exasperation washed over the front of the little girl's pink tee shirt.

"Kirsten, maybe you should put on the red shoes. That witch is scared of those things. Get the shoes, Kirsten! C'mon, before Mom gets here."

Charlotte appeared at the playroom doorway. "Oh, girls, it's not that damn Ozzzz.com site again! Shut that thing off now, I say!"

"Mommy, we can't go till she's dead! We can't. She won't leave us alone. Please, please, help us kill her," cried Amanda.

Charlotte collapsed into the bright blue beanbag chair in the corner of the room. "Girls, I don't think I can. I just don't think I know how to kill her!"

"The 21st century technologies — genetics, nanotechnology, and robotics (GNR) — are so powerful that they can spawn whole new classes of accidents and abuses. Most dangerously, for the first time, these accidents and abuses are widely within the reach of individuals or small groups. They will not require large facilities or rare raw materials. Knowledge alone will enable the use of them."

Wired Magazine, April 2000, "Why the Future Doesn't Need Us" by Bill Joy

Chapter 1

Boys 'n the Wood

"It's a beautiful thing we're creating, Avi," said Sam. "And I've found a way to make the idea irresistible to him."

Avi, steadfast and unshakable like Mount Sinai, stood next to Sam, shoulder to shoulder in a clearing encircled by the old-growth Northern California redwood trees that shrouded the secrets of the Woodlands Club. The two men were a few hundred feet from the lodge. It looked like everyone had cleared out after breakfast. They wanted to make sure that the dining hall was empty, that there would be no eavesdroppers around during their meeting with Portell.

Bob Portell appeared at the appointed time and swung open the huge wooden doors, disappearing inside.

"Wait. Let's give it a few minutes," said Sam.

Avi nodded. Sam glanced at him. The eight-inch scar that ran down from the top of Avi's ear to the base of his neck bulged like a mountain ridge on a topo map in the unforgiving glare. That man is raw chutzpah, thought Sam.

"Yah, Sam, and we'll make it impossible for that bastard to resist. We'll have him on his knees, groveling, in no time. My gun is loaded." The Israeli fighter pilot adjusted the black patch over his left eye and patted his bulging chest. "And you, Sam?"

"Avi, I'm stoked." Sam was jazzed, feeling optimum, at his peak after a ten-mile morning run through the serpentine trails of the Woodlands complex, a round of Zen longevity calisthenics, and then, of course, last night with the club's head hostess, Carmelita, his Caribbean Queen. And what a hostess she was! *Mmmm. Mmmm. That creamy dark chocolate skin!*

Sam paused for a moment to check his watch. Perfect timing. Ten minutes late. Late enough to let Portell know who was really running this gig, but not too late to let the pretentious fool think that Sam was jerking his chain. Sam knew he had to tread carefully. But he also knew that he was clever enough to have Portell wrapped around his little finger in a snap. This was an opportunity that Sam couldn't afford to miss. This was the proverbial brass ring. Sam wanted it so bad, it made him ache, and he would use every trick he had acquired in the course of his business career to one up Portell. Of course, if things got rough, he could always count on Avi to put it all back on track. In Sam's mind, there was only one agenda, as always—his own.

Avi and Sam approached the entrance to the Woodlands main lodge, a sprawling robust structure hewn from stones and logs, where most of the meals and strategy sessions took place. Sam swung open the massive doors carved with the emblem of The Woodlands Club—the raptor eagle with a small furry creature in its talons.

He spied Bob Portell hunched over his coffee at the far end of one of the six thirty-foot long redwood tables in the dining hall. Everything was in place. Sam noted that Carmelita was on duty. He walked over to her and slipped his arm around her waist, whispering words that evoked a reassuring nod, a wink and a knowing smile from her. *Done deal.* She would wait on their table, as they discussed last night.

It looked like the breakfast crowd had indeed cleared out. They were probably in the grove or at the amphitheater participating in the annual Spring Rites competitions and festivities. Good thing, too, thought Sam. *We don't need any of the other global moguls nosing in on this. If they want it, they'll have to bleed their bank accounts, and then some, to get it.*

Sam savored the whole scene. He had finally made the grade. Sam was now fully integrated into the elite corps after a decade of persistently hammering the top echelons of the global-corporate elite with his mantra about the power of the technologies he was promoting. For one week in the spring, during the equinox, Sam walked among the best of breed—billionaire CEOs, sheiks, prime ministers, media moguls, superstars, intellectuals and leaders of fringe terrorist groups who converged upon this pristine redwood grove north of San Francisco to hatch their schemes, to seal deals, and unabashedly share their ruthless machinations with their like-minded brethren. And now Sam was one of the stars.

Sam and Avi sat down on the long, picnic-style bench, strategically flanking Bob Portell. *Geez, for all of his billions, you'd think he'd hire an image consultant! The guy's a bloody disaster! That unironed L.L. Bean flannel shirt has got to go! And those hideous baggy chinos! Get a clue, Portell!* Ever since Sam had known him from the garage shop days, Bob couldn't get over the rumpled geek look.

Sam waved to Carmelita, who took the cue and waltzed up to the trio and leaned over, inches away from Portell. Her cloud of African curls brushed against Bob's cheek while she recited the brunch specials. Sam chuckled as he watched Bob slide a few inches away from her.

"So, Mr. Portell, what's your pleasure?" Carmelita smiled, laying her hand softly on his shoulder. They were practically nose to nose.

"Oh, uh, a cheese omelet with gourmet cornbread."

Bob twitched uncomfortably, relieved when Carmelita had finished taking everyone's orders and finally removed herself from his personal space.

Good girl! thought Sam. *Check out Portell's body English! Got a problem with kinky hair, boy?*

Bob collected himself. Sam enjoyed baiting Portell. With Portell's bid for the presidential seat, any revelations about his family's involvement in the genetic purification movement during the forties and fifties could spell disaster for the liberal vote.

"Let's get down to business," said Bob.

"Bob, it's ready to go. Yah, in only thirty days we'll be pressing all their buttons until they crack. I can't imagine anything more elegant. It's the subtlety that is so appealing to me!" Avi smiled.

"All right, all right, guys. Let's cut to the chase," snapped Bob, wiping his mouth with his sleeve. "Don't waste my time. You say that you can engineer a shift in mass consciousness with this technology. That's all I care about."

"Bob, you saw the prototype. It's a masterpiece. It burrows down into their minds and souls, and they won't even know what hit them. What do you not understand about global domination?"

"Yah, what's your problem anyway?" Avi jumped up from his seat and pounded the table with his fist, rattling Portell's coffee cup. "Can't you recognize beauty when you see it? It's a revolution in communication, Goddamit! Primal-speak over the 'Net. It doesn't matter who they are, where they come from, or what their IQ is! Don't you get it?"

"Avi, get a grip, my man! Bob, you will be all over it. It's a one-shot deal too. No programming, no deprogramming. Ever! Your word will rule. Your message bites will be sucked into the reptilian brains of the populace, and you, of all people, know how that handy piece of anatomy works. You'll have them licking your boots in nanoseconds!"

"You guys know that I'm from Missouri," said Bob. "Show me. Results talk, bullshit walks."

"Bob, I'm telling you, you'll be all over it. I'm testing it out on the Ozzzz.com site as we speak. You'll be lord and master of the cyber class in no time."

"Yah, guaranteed! And if it doesn't work, we can still resort to the old kamikaze tactics. Direct hits have always appealed to me!" quipped Avi.

"Avi, stop being such a damn yahoo!" responded Bob. "Okay, Sam. I want to hear how you're going to pull this off, and then maybe I'll consider it."

"It's already in the works. We're ready to roll with Ozzzz.com," explained Sam. "We've already got over a million subscribers. The site's been running for a few months, and we've got the metrics. We're golden, I'm telling you."

"Can't you see it now! The new tagline: 'Move beyond mind share to mind control.' It's beautiful! So beautiful!" said Avi.

"Okay, I think I get the picture. So you prove your point. Then what? Why should I give a shit?" asked Bob.

"The 'then what,' Bob is in your hands. You'll have the whole world in your hands, bro'! Just imagine what this could do for the head of state. Taste it, Bob! Taste it! Hail to the chief!"

"All right, I'll back you up on this exercise, but to actually spread this stuff over the Internet globally, I've gotta see results. Stats. Numbers. Concrete evidence. Get it, Sam? I'm not a dreamer, I'm a billionaire."

"We're on, my man. Hey, look, guys, I have to run. There are some new hires coming in. And there's one in particular I want to snag—smart, and quite a babe too."

"Keep me posted. And, hey, Sam, next time, could you get this place to assign a different waitress to us, like that little blonde over by the bar. This one gave me the willies."

"Bob, you'll get every damn thing you need and want, on my word. You understand my MO," Sam reassured him. "And, by the way, you might consider drawing on some talent in the industry to fill some of those key cabinet posts, if you get my drift."

"Yah, if Henry Kissinger could do it, why not me?" bellowed the Israeli. "Hey, for Americans, you fellas are not such schlemiels!"

"Greed is good"

Gordon Gekko, from the movie "Wall Street"

Chapter 2

An Offer You Can't Refuse

Caitlin. Ahhh, Caitlin. The perfect pedigree. The perfect profile. Oh, baby, I've had my eye on you for a while. A face that could launch a thousand websites. They will eat you up, my digital darling!

Sam checked his e-mail. He smiled at the subject heading in the first e-mail from Tinker: Slam Dunk!

Mime-Version: 1.0
Date: Tues, 21 Mar 2000 12:58:16 -0800
To: sthorne@ozzzz.com
From: Guy Tinker <gtinker@ozzzz.com>
Subject: Slam Dunk
Status:

Sam,
I'm moving in on the kill. Should be able to bag 'er within 24 hours. Six-figures, 100,000 shares, full-package, perks, and fringes. I'll touch base with HR this morning to clinch it.

Tinker

Date: Tues., 21 Mar 2000 13:28:00 -0800
From: st <sthorne@ozzzz.com>
Reply-To: gtinker@ozzzz.com
X-Accept-Language: en
MIME-Version: 1.0
To: Sam Thorne <sthorne@ozzzz.com>
Subject: Re: Slamdunk
Status:

Tink,

Whatever it takes. This one's mission-critical. Buzz me on the cell this aft.

$am

Mime-Version: 1.0
Date: Tues, 21 Mar 2000 13:58:16 -0800
To: sailorsshanty@safetynet.com
From: Katherine Rainier <krainier@ozzzz.com>
Subject: We extend our welcome
Status:

Dear Caitlin,
On behalf of Sam Thorne, CEO, I am pleased to offer you the position of Director of Web Technology at Ozzzz.com. We propose the following salary and benefits, based on your qualifications:

- Annual Salary; $165,000.

- Stock Options: 100,000 shares @$.50 per share vested over four years.

- Benefits: 100% medical, dental and vision coverage, subsidized employee cafeteria, 24-hour access to fitness facilities and Ozzzz-zone gaming room, 4 weeks vacation annually, 100% employer subsidized continuing education, flex-time and telecommuting option, one-month paid corporate housing, company car.

- Perks: 5 free round-trip flights anywhere in the U.S.

We sincerely hope that you accept this offer and join the exciting world of Ozzzz.com. Should you decide to join our company, your starting date would be Monday, April 1. Please reply via e-mail or fax.

Best regards,
Katherine Rainier, Director of Human Resources

Mime-Version: 1.0
Date: Tues, 21 Mar 2000 16:04:16 -0800
To: sthorne@ozzzz.com
From: Guy Tinker <gtinker@ozzzz.com>
Subject: Hooked
Status:

Sam,

She bit.

I'll ring you later.

Tink

"We have come to claim our promise, O Oz."

From The Wonderful Wizard of Oz, by Frank Baum, originally published in 1900.

Chapter 3

<u>www.ozzzz.com</u>

Download RealPlayer audio.

"Welcome, Caitlin. We're so happy to have you back again. The last time we saw you was too long ago! February 28, 2000. We've missed you, and look forward to spending even more time with you today! So leave your worries behind and come join us at the incredible, funtabulous, marvelistic, e-stounding world of Ozzzz.com!"

Point. Good Witch. Bad Witch. Click.

Flying blue monkeys careening across the screen, screeching menacingly.

Can you outrun them in your ruby red slippers? Drag your ruby reds and drop them over a monkey for instant annihilation. No time to pause and take a breath. The Wicked Witch of the West presses her green, wart-studded face up against your monitor. "You don't have much longer, my pretty!" Dragging and dropping your ruby reds over the Wicked Witch results in loss of the coveted slippers. More flying blue monkeys come at you chaotically from all directions. No defenses left. But wait, a tiny bucket of water flashes in the midst of the melee. Drag it down to your corner. Wait for your opportunity. The pointy-hatted Nemesis comes into view and disappears in a flash. This requires ultra-fast reflexes. There she is again. Splash. Decimated. Munchkins populate the screen. "Heigh-ho the witch is dead. Heigh-ho, the Wicked Witch is dead!"

Exit game, click on "Home" button.

Point. Ozzzz.com Scorecard. Click.

Up pops a scoresheet with the number of points you've accumulated playing games on Ozzzz.com. One dead Wicked Witch of the West is worth 500 points. One flying blue monkey only 10.

2,500 points gets you 25% off the Ozzzz.com CD-ROM Game Pack.

Click here to order. Your Ozzzz.com account will be automatically billed.

Point. Join us for Teatime with the Tinman Online! Click. Enter chatroom.

"Dear Tinman, who is the real Wizard? Some of the kids at school say that there's no such thing as Santa Claus. I don't believe them. Can you please tell us the truth?"

"I heard that the Wizard is really a woman, like the Good Witch of the North."

"Then, she must be awesome! So smart, so beautiful!"

"Where do you live? How old are you? I'm 9, and I don't live in Kansas like Dorothy. I live in Illinois. Near Chicago. I just ordered the new Glinda and Wicked Witch robo dolls, and they're to die for!"

"Hey, Tinman, how come I don't have to wait for your games to come up on the screen like I do on all the other game Websites? You must be a supernatural programmer! This is the best kid's site on the planet!"

"Mom's yelling at me to come to dinner. I really don't want to go, but if I don't, she'll cut me off. Bye, munchkins! Bye, Tinman!"

"I want to know why we never get to see Dorothy up close, only her ruby red slippers? I want to meet the real Dorothy soon! I want to be just like her! My mom even bought me the Virtual Dorothy pigtails and dress costume!"

Exit Teatime with the Tinman Online.

Point. Children's E-ducation Fund. Click.

Video. CEO of Ozzzz.com. No tie. Big smile. Handsome and sincere.

"Hi, I'm Sam Thorne of Ozzzz.com. Every time you or your parents visit this magical land of Ozzzz.com, every time you purchase one of our many extraordinary entertaining and educational products, 20% of the proceeds go to our 'Children's E-ducation Fund.' This fund is my way of providing educational opportunities for children less fortunate than you across the globe. The fund provides computers and instruction so that financially-challenged children can develop and refine the skills they'll need to meet the future head-on with confidence. At Ozzzz.com, we believe that the future is in the hands of our young people and we have dedicated ourselves wholeheartedly to that vision. Thank-you for being a member of our global community!"

Exit.

Point upper left-hand corner. Shut down browser.

Wow! Unbelievable! Technology with values. That's the place for me. With that, Caitlin opened up her e-mail application and composed her acceptance note to the Director of Human Resources at Ozzzz.com. *Silicon Valley, I'm all yours!*

"I think it is no exaggeration to say we are on the cusp of the further perfection of extreme evil, an evil whose possibility spreads well beyond that which weapons of mass destruction bequeathed to the nation-states, on to a surprising and terrible empowerment of extreme individuals."

Wired Magazine, April 2000, "Why the Future Doesn't Need Us" by Bill Joy

Chapter 4

Initiation

The 747 jumbo jet dipped down below cloud level. Caitlin's heartbeat spiked as she turned to look out the window. The sparkling blue waters of the San Francisco Bay and the jeweled city zoomed in towards her. She was almost home! *My new home! It looks even more beautiful than Maine!*

As the pilot announced that the plane was preparing for landing, Caitlin secured her tray table and put her reading material in her lap. She had just finished reading the cover story in *Wired Magazine*, "The Soul of Silicon Valley," featuring Sam Thorne's newest enterprise, Ozzzz.com.

The middle-aged businessman seated next to her peered over to see what she had been reading. He was tall and tan with an outdoorsy look. The woman he was with was a slender, dark-haired woman with a warm, inviting smile. They had a fresh, relaxed quality about them that appealed to Caitlin.

"Oh, God, Mariel," he said to his partner, pointing to Sam's photo on the magazine cover. "Do you believe this guy? What a self-promoter!"

"Well, Greg, nothing that man comes up with surprises me. We both know what a snake he is!" commented Mariel.

"Excuse me, Miss, but would you mind if we take a quick look at your *Wired Magazine*? By the way, I'm Greg, and this is my partner, Mariel."

"Pleased to meet you. Caitlin Leary," said Caitlin, handing him the magazine. "By the way, I couldn't help overhearing your comments. You two don't seem to have a very high opinion of Sam Thorne."

"Anyone that's worked for Sam can tell you that he's a master deceiver and manipulator."

"What do you mean?" asked Caitlin, puzzled by Greg's negativity.

"Look, about five years ago, we were brought into Sam's huge database development company, Prophet Corporation—I'm sure you know it well—to do an organizational audit. He was having attrition and morale problems, so he wanted to get a handle on how to cope. The gist of the story is that we initiated in-depth interviews with key employees in just about every division, and I can tell you, that there was more than dissension and discontent in the ranks, having almost nothing to do with compensation, I might add," explained Greg.

"Really? So, what was going on? I've heard nothing but great things about the new venture, Ozzzz.com," said Caitlin. "In fact, I just accepted a position there. It sure seems like it's an incredible way of using technology for the public good."

"Well, without saying too much—and this is strictly confidential— let's just say that a number of the employees we spoke with had some major concerns about Prophet's business practices. The sad part of it all is that I doubt that they ever used any of the information we researched for them. But, that's business. At any rate, I only hope that you don't fall into false idealism for the sake of your well- being. You seem like a good kid. I'd hate to see you get hurt. Watch out for that guy. He's slick and slimy, and he's got a thing for smart, pretty women like you," advised Greg, returning the magazine to Caitlin. "Keep your guard up, that's what I would recommend."

The jet's belly smacked the runway hard, jostling the passengers. After the plane came to an abrupt stop, Caitlin collected herself and took a deep breath. *I have to digest this.* Holding the rolled up magazine in her hand, she waved good-bye to Greg and Mariel as they disappeared into the crowd.

"Due to improved techniques the elite will have greater control over the masses; and because human work will no longer be necessary, the masses will be superfluous, a useless burden on the system. If the elite is ruthless, they may simply decide to exterminate the mass of humanity. If they are humane, they may use propaganda or other psychological or biological techniques to reduce the birth rate until the mass of humanity becomes extinct, leaving the world to the elite."

From Drawing Life...Surviving the Unabomber by Theodore Kaczynski

Chapter 5

Casting Pearls

"Open up your palm, Sam," said Avi, who filled Sam's open hand with a mound of tiny crystalline bead-like particles, each about the size of a grain of rice.

Sam's eyes dilated as he carefully selected one of the microchips and held it up to the light emitted by the halogen lamp on his desk.

"Amazing. Fully programmable nanocomputers, scaled down to such a minute size as to be barely noticeable. Yah, small is beauti-ful!" commented Avi. "And eminently wearable," he added, as he spilled the contents of his briefcase onto the surface of Sam's desk...necklaces, bracelets, rings, earrings, key chains, finger pup-pets, watches, refrigerator magnets, collectible cards, and assorted charms, all bearing the distinct Ozzzz.com logo mark.

Sam pulled out a magnifying glass from his top desk drawer and inspected a few of the items. He pulled the faux purple amethyst off of a cheap silver ring, and a small crystal grain popped out. He ripped the hat off of a finger puppet that looked like the Tin Man, and another small bead popped out. He tore open the two pieces of thick stock that were glued together to form the two sides of a collector's card and found a grain stuck to one of the adhesive surfaces.

"Very underhanded, surreptitious, and downright sneaky! I love it! Stealth marketing at it's best. Okay, Avi, don't tell me. I get it! We can program these little suckers with our messages and emit the wave patterns of the thoughtforms through these cute little thingamabobs. We'll get them coming and going. Once the Fed Ex packages show up at their doors, they'll be completely mesmerized by Ozzzz.com. The little voices inside their puny little consumer brains will continue to beg them to buy, buy, and buy more! You're a friggin' genius!"

"Yah, but wait, Sam. We are barely scratching the surface. There is huge potential here for even more. I have a lab full of genetic engineers working with chip designers back in Haifa, implementing a programmable DNA module. We're focusing on scalability right now. If you think these are small, wait till we roll out the new pro-totypes. We are designing them to be the size of a poppy seed. Of course, you'll be able to program them with messages that can be transmitted electromagnetically! And the big bonus is that you'll also be able to get these tiny chips to speak the language of the double helix. In other words, programmable genetic engineering. They can be swallowed, injected, inserted into food even! Can you think of anything that a certain power-hungry presidential candidate would covet more? Especially one whose family has a fascination for genetic purification?"

"Whoa, Avi. This is mind-boggling. But do we really want Portell to get his mitts on this?"

"Sam, as you well know, from business as well as, er, your personal adventures—promise them anything they want to hear, but give them nothing."

"You're dead on, Avi. Seduce 'em and then pick up and leave 'em in the dust, panting after you."

"Help Wanted

...Over the past three years, Microsoft has contributed more than $570 million in financial, product, and training support to help America develop more skilled workers. This includes our recent contribution of $344 million in software to support Intel's Teach the Future program, a worldwide effort to train more than 400,000 classroom teachers how to use technology to enhance learning; and $73 million to the United Negro College Fund to improve computer access and training for students and faculty members at historically black colleges and universities nationwide."

Microsoft © 2000 Microsoft Corporation

Ad from the San Jose Mercury News, Wednesday, April 5, 2000, following a federal judge's antitrust ruling against Microsoft.

Chapter 6

Pride and Prejudice

Sam felt the pulsing of his microhandheld in his jeans pocket. It must be Mo. He pulled out the device and flicked on the miniature monitor. Mo's face, about the size of a postage stamp, smiled back at him and said, "Hey, Sam, I'm outside, reporting for duty."

Sam walked over to his security monitor panel and buzzed in Mo. Mo passed through the wired, double-gated front door of Sam's megahome, a perpetual work-in-progress that he had christened "Shambala." Since the first boulder was dropped in place by the feng shui master from Nanking, the place was constantly populated by construction crews, landscapers, architects, and living-space consultants. Today was an exception. Sam gave everyone the day off.

Sam offered Mo a warm, manly hug. Sam had a soft spot in his heart for Mo. Mo was one of the few people that Sam felt he could ever trust in his entire life. *You're my kind of people, Mo!* That became clear in the early days when Sam craved his white powder, which fueled his drive to succeed, and Mo always came through for him with the best stuff money could buy. Mo always stood

beside him, never questioning his motives or his actions.
He was a tactician's dream, the supreme lieutenant, cut from the
same cloth.

"Mo, it's one of those incredible California days. Why don't we
relax in the Zen garden. I have got a super-important mission for
you. Hey, can I fix *you* a drink for a change?"

"Great idea. Just a Coke over ice."

"Still keeping out of trouble, then, Mo?"

"You got it. That's not changin' for the rest of my life. No more
drinkin' for me. Gotta keep myself on track. You know how that
one goes."

Sam smiled at the comment, remembering his own high-flying
days when a mirror and a rolled up thousand-dollar bill were as
indispensable as his cell-phone was today. The duo walked down
a broad sweep of a corridor that opened out into a manicured
Japanese garden. Mo sat down at an ornately carved Tibetan table
that overlooked a reflecting pool stocked with giant goldfish that
fluttered through the pristine water, free from errant leaves.

Situated behind the table was an immense Tibetan Buddha lost in
serene contemplation. The feng shui master had discovered the ten-
foot statue in a tiny monastery in Lhasa. It was said to have special
powers, bringing fame and adulation to those who offered their
prayers and intentions. Sam walked around the back of the statue.
Pulling out his microhandheld, he typed in a code. A rectangular
hunk of stone slid over to the left to reveal a combination bar and

refrigeration unit where he could store cold drinks and snacks for his guests. Sam poured a couple of Cokes and joined Mo at the table.

"Mo, I have a special assignment for you. It's right up your alley. There's no slack on this one, no leeway. You'll be handsomely rewarded for execution, and if you fuck up, well, I can't even begin to tell you what the repercussions might be for all of us. You, me, your kids out in Florida. We're all at risk. Are you game?"

"Sam, you know me. Yeah, I'm game. I'll do anything. I've been through just about every kinda hell known to mankind. How bad can it be? Just tell me what's in it for me, and we'll talk."

"Good. We always see eye to eye, don't we, my man! Here's what's in it for you—five hundred grand, cash, and 50,000 shares of founder's stock options in Ozzzz.com. Is that worth your while? The cash'll tide you over for a while, and you won't have to worry about educating your kids—you can buy Alabama State when you cash in your options. The price per share was $234 at close yesterday."

"Sam, I think I can put my hand out for that one. So, what do I gotta do? One thing I'm drawin' the line on—I'll do no physical harm to any livin' thing."

"Hey, Mo, who are you talking to? You know me better than that. My hands have always been clean that way. No worries, my man. This is straight up. I want to tap into your racial pride."

"What are you talkin' about, my racial pride? "

"Mo, how much have you suffered in your own life because of your skin color? How much pain have your parents and grand-parents had to endure silently because of their heritage?"

"Sam, I'm tryin' to forget all that, 'cause if I keep thinkin' about it all the time, I'm apt to create some pretty nasty scenarios. I'm not in Birmingham any more. I'm sittin' here in a temple in Woodside. I'm done with the past."

"Well, can I just ask you to remember, just a little? Just touch that place inside of you where there might be a vestige of resentment and anger. You know what I'm saying? I need for you to go back to that place in order for us to implement my plan."

"Yeah? How's that? You want me to become angry and militant so that you can do your business? That makes no sense to me! What are you talkin' about?"

"Mo, let me lay it all out for you. You know who Bob Portell is. He's got something I need. He's got the 'Net wrapped up in his browser and online ad tools. I need to sell him on something, something that will revolutionize the way the world thinks and works. Something that'll revolutionize the way your kids function in the world."

"Okay, I'll buy that. He's got something you want, and you want me to help you get it. But what's that got to do with my racial pride, anyway? How the heck do you expect someone like me to convince a billionaire with a high IQ to open up his kimono to you? D'you think he'd listen to me—I'm a sanitation engineer. This is crazy!"

"Not at all. I'm about to tell you something that's not widely known about Bob and the Portell family. It's been kept hush-hush, covered-up, whitewashed for decades, and, believe me, it's not something that Portell would want splashed across the 'Net or the nightly news. Mo, you and your family are from down South. Remember how back in the 50's the Portells funded a family planning center in Alabama? The center was touted as a community resource designed to help poor ethnic minorities—native Americans and especially blacks—with family planning and parenthood issues. Well, it was all a ruse. In fact, the Portells were instrumental in spearheading the genetic purification movement in this country, shortly after World War II. The center in Alabama was really set up as a lab that carried on experiments for population reduction of non-Aryan races."

"Sam, are you puttin' me on? I don't believe this! I just don't believe this! I kinda do remember that place, though. My pa and grandpa went over there for vasectomy operations, and they told me how they had to keep going back all the time for some kind of injections just so that the operation wouldn't reverse itself."

"I think you're getting the picture, Mo. Sterilization was only one means of stemming the population. The other was outright germ warfare. They injected your folks with everything from syphilis to mutating cancer cells."

"Jeez, Sam, I don't believe you're tellin' me this. I get you now. Yeah, racial pride. Yeah, I can kick that in pretty quick. That Portell's got a nerve showin' off like he's some kind of charitable benefactor. It's bullshit. It's all lies and bullshit. I almost wish I could blow the goddam geek's cover, but I know you've got your thing to do and I gotta make sure my kids have a future. So, look, Sam, I'll do whatever, and I'll take the compensation. Any chance you could front me some of that now?"

"Here, take this," Sam reached into his pocket and produced a wad of thousands. *Mo, I knew you'd come through for me. We're bros, aren't we? Through and through.*" All you need to do is intimidate the hell out of him, okay? Scare the living daylights out of him...like you know it all and you're going to talk, till I put the full court press on him. Okay? I'll give you further instructions in a few days. And don't forget, Mo, you are under oath. You know what that means."

"Sam, I think I'm touchin' that place inside of me!"

"Her eyes closed in spite of herself and she forgot where she was and fell among the poppies, fast asleep."

From The Wonderful Wizard of Oz, by Frank Baum, originally published in 1900.

Chapter 7

Welcome to the Ozzzz-Zone

Caitlin was greeted in the lobby by a lanky, doe-eyed Indian man with a wide, toothy grin.

"Hi, Caitlin, I'm Rajit, or Raj, as the Americans call me. I'm your 'buddy' today. You know, to show you around and all that." Raj spoke with a slight English accent overlaying his Bombay lilt.

Caitlin warmed up to Raj immediately. *At least he's not some gnome-like geek with pizza breath!*

Rajit led her through security. He spoke his name and the vast voice-activated double doors painted in faux gilt flung open. They had entered the Emerald City.

This is more incredible than I could ever have imagined! Caitlin's eyes widened. The place looked like a combination of a rave dance hall—with images flashing rapidly on huge screens suspended from the 50-foot ceiling—and a surreal techno-city of the future. There was no relief from stimulation anywhere.

Raj herded her over to a round domed room in the middle of the building. "This is the Ozzzz-Zone. It's sort of a decompression chamber. Here you can recharge your batteries. There's everything from espresso to 250,000 MP3 music titles to listen to. There are games, smart drinks, and even a coed hot tub."

I've never seen anything like this. In the large main chamber, splayed out on purple, orange, and lime green floor pillows were bodies of all descriptions. Some of them wore virtual reality goggles, while others had on just headphones and herbal eye pillows. Once in a while, Caitlin heard a guffaw or incomprehensible utterances that sounded vaguely like singing that spilled forth from one of the bodies. In another area, she saw clusters of geeks huddled over huge monitors, completely engrossed in games like Quake,™ Riven,™ Unreal,™ or new games created at Ozzzz.com that had not yet been released for public consumption on the Internet. In the hot tub tucked behind a dark wall blazing with neon tube lights, Caitlin noticed a trio of pale, thin young men in Ozzzz.com swim trunks discussing the merits of the Java programming language. The whole scene reminded her of a Year 2000 interpretation of a Hieryonomous Bosch triptych that she would have named "Geek Purgatory."

As they left the decompression chamber, Caitlin vowed silently never to set foot in the Ozzzz-Zone.

Next on the agenda were the welcome kit and her office. In the land of Ozzzz.com, some had cubicles and the lucky few had offices. She lucked out. Her office even had a window, except that it did not look out on the real world. Caitlin peered through the glass and took in the view, a virtual reality depiction of a lush garden, complete with waterfalls and fairy sprites.

On her desk was a large picnic basket with a note on it.

Caitlin, this is your welcome kit to get you off to a flying start. Your e-mail and phone account have already been set up. All you need to do is dial #15 and speak your name 5 times so that the voice recognition security system learns your name. We don't believe in dog tags here. To get into the building, just speak your name, like I did earlier, and 'Open Sesame!' Why don't you spend some time settling in? I'll check in with you again around noon.

Caitlin opened her welcome kit. It contained:

A 32 oz. Ozzzz.com coffee mug

A green plastic squirt gun molded in the shape of a winged dragon

A polo shirt with the Ozzzz.com logo tastefully embroidered on the left side.

A half-dozen packets of instant hot chocolate

A bottle of Jolt

Several half-price coupons for Pizza Hut

And the gadgets, of course:

A Blackberry™ interactive e-mail pager

A cell phone

A PalmPilot™

A full-scale laptop computer with carrying case

Caitlin tried out her ergonomically correct Aeron™ chair. It felt as if it had been molded to her fit the contours of her body perfectly. Ummm, really comfy. She swiveled around a few times and decided to check her e-mail. After logging on, she was greeted with a voice-mail message—several bars of a digital rendition of "Over the Rainbow" followed by Sam Thorne's personal welcome to the land of Ozzzz.com. Caitlin pinched herself. This is not a dream. I'm really here!

"While she stood looking eagerly at the strange and beautiful sights, she noticed coming toward her a group of the queerest people she had ever seen."

From The Wonderful Wizard of Oz, by Frank Baum, originally published in 1900.

Chapter 8

The Emerald City Diner

Raj reappeared at Caitlin's office precisely at noon. "Sam's waiting for you in his private dining room, Caitlin."

Caitlin followed Raj's lead. He guided her down the expansive warehouse complex to the Emerald City Diner. *This is no ordinary subsidized cafeteria*, thought Caitlin. It was a gourmet cornucopia, with choices ranging from steaming hot Thainese noodle soup to mounds of saffron-laced Moroccan couscous, to hearty Yankee comfort food covered with gravy.

The diner was divided into at least a dozen different ethnic eateries, each with its own distinct ambience and interactive kiosk ordering stations at each table, where employees entered their choices. Servers, mostly Hispanic or Asian immigrants, filled the orders and brought meals to the Ozzzz.com e-lite.

Caitlin and Raj walked through an archway toward an ornate octagonal structure with onion-shaped domes reminiscent of the Taj Mahal. Raj waved his hand, and two ornate doors slowly opened into a softly lit room draped with silk saris in rich jewel colors.

"Caitlin, welcome to Ozzzz.com!" said Sam, who was seated yogi-style on a thickly padded brocade cushion. "I hope you like Indian food. It reminds me of perfume—a true culinary and sensory delight. As Raj can tell you, our cuisine is the real thing, right Raj?"

Raj smiled and nodded. "Almost as good as my mother's cooking— quite awesome, in fact."

"Come, Caitlin, make yourself comfortable. And, Raj, many thanks, Saheeb!" Raj bowed in mock ceremony and made his exit.

Caitlin sank into a saffron-colored embroidered cushion next to Sam. In front of them was a round marble tabletop with a monitor inlaid in the center. Three-dimensional images of savory Indian dishes floated in and out of view, accompanied by mouth-watering aromas that wafted through the entire room.

"Our virtual reality programming team hasn't quite perfected the sense of taste yet, so we'll have to leave that to our palates for now. What's your pleasure? You can just point to the dish that looks and smells appealing to you."

Caitlin pointed to the curried chicken with rice, dal, and hot chai. The savory aromas wafted into the room.

"Check this out. See this tiny little icon over here, the one that looks like a pair of red shoes? If I touch it, I can survey the entire dining room. Here, let's have a look at the scene. Mind you, I don't do this very often!" said Sam.

Sam lightly touched the icon and the food displays faded out, replaced by scenes of people milling around the various ethnic food kiosks in the Emerald City diner.

"So here's a sociological snapshot of Ozzzz.com, Caitlin. MBAs over there at the sushi bar, the suits—sales reps and sales managers—at the grill, GenXers in their beloved black uniforms picking at the salad bar, and the 'geris,' the older techies, at the Italian bistro. There you have it! The five-second tour!"

"Interesting," said Caitlin. For a moment, she flashed back to the conversation she had in the airplane with the management consultants. *This is a little eerie. I wonder if he has surveillance equipment all over the building? Well, maybe he's just trying to impress me.* "So where do you hide the cameras? I know that if they're small enough, they're pretty imperceptible. With nanotechnology, you can build them so that they're really tiny, like seeds, or even smaller."

"Oh sure! But, hey, let's turn this thing off and talk about you. That's why we're here. And it looks like lunch has arrived," said Sam. The door opened and two young men in turbans and loose silk trousers floated into the room balancing large silver trays bearing fragrant Indian food. As they were setting the dishes on the table, Sam adjusted his position on the cushion and drew in a little closer to Caitlin.

"Well, Caitlin, I want to officially welcome you to Ozzzz.com! I can't tell you how delighted and lucky we are that you chose to join our organization. You know, after reviewing your profile, I can't help but think that you could contribute in so many different ways to our cause."

"I would be honored to help in any way possible. Mr. Thorne, I was reading the article in *Wired* on the plane, and I couldn't help but admire the way you've successfully used technology to serve education on a global level. I'm the one who is honored. I'm so grateful to be here, and I'd be thrilled to help in any way I can."

"What a stellar attitude!" beamed Sam. "One of the ideas we've toyed with here is having a spokesperson for the kids. You know, a role model, someone that they could look up to. Right now, we have all of these animated characters, Virtual Dorothy and the rest. I'd really like to see a real live human grace the pages of our website, someone who really speaks to the children, someone who really inspires them," said Sam. "Oh, and here, you must try this incredible lamb. Perfection!"

Sam lifted a forkful of lamb up to Caitlin's lips.

What am I supposed to do? Okay, I guess I'll have to eat it. He's the CEO, after all. It would be rude not to. Geez, it's my first day, and I can't mess up! I better go along with this. They never taught us about how to deal with this in graduate school! Caitlin leaned toward Sam and opened her mouth to receive the bite of his lunch and gulped it down a little too quickly. She chased it down with a sip of spicy sweet chai.

"Oh, yeah. Good. I mean the lamb—and the idea. That sure sounds like a great idea. Maybe we can get a celebrity sponsor! Do you have anyone in mind yet?" asked Caitlin nervously shoving her food into small piles on her plate. Her appetite had left her.

"Well, I do have my eye on one particular individual," he said, laying his hand on her forearm and leaning even closer yet, as if sharing a well-kept secret. "I can't quite disclose that information yet, but you'll be the first one to know, Caitlin. After all, as Director of Web Technology you'll be intimately involved in setting up live webcasts and streaming video, of course."

"I'm up for that and anything else that will make Ozzzz.com the best educational resource on the Internet!" said Caitlin, straightening up.

"Well, it's all up to you, Caitlin. I have utter and complete confidence in you. I expect great things from you, and I have no reason to doubt that your performance will be anything less than spellbinding! So, why don't we plan another pow-wow? Jot down some of your thoughts, your dreams, where you see us going in six months, and we can put our heads together. Is that a deal, Caitlin?"

"We're on, Mr. Thorne!"

"Ah, ah! Sam. Caitlin, this is Silicon Valley—no formalities here! We are all collaborators in this! All co-creators of the Ozzzz.com experience. Don't ever forget that! Look, I have a meeting, and I know you're anxious to settle in. I'll catch up with you in a few days."

Caitlin pushed herself away from the marble table and stood up to take her leave. As she walked through the double doors of the Taj Mahal, she felt something harden in the pit of her belly.

"Technology is a woman's best friend. It's served me well, and I swear by it, for everything you need and want in life—from a perfect profile to a perfect portfolio."

Bambi Rose

Chapter 9

Buffalo's

Every weekday morning, rain, shine, earthquake or mudslide, Bambi Rose perched herself strategically at her favorite table in the far corner of Buffalo's café. Positioning was everything. It was the best spot for lingering over a latte, taking in the scene, and intentionally ensuring that she would not be overlooked by anyone who walked in.

Over the years, having cashed in on her options many times over, Bambi had earned the title of "Digital Diva," an angel investor who swooped in on any innovative "e-idea" that came along. It wasn't a question of amassing more riches. Bambi was addicted to the game. It gave her life juice and purpose. It made her significant. And, above all, she fed on the drama.

In the early days of Silicon Valley, Bambi learned to flaunt her Ivy-league MBA and her looks. Thanks to Dad, she was fixed up with the best plastic surgeons in the business. Flitting from start-up to start-up, Bambi was on the move and on the make—a silicone sister in search of a Silicon Mister. Twenty years later after a string of dalliances with CEOs, CFOs, and COOs, Bambi settled for an occasional fling with young programmers eager to lose their inno-cence and slam-dunk their first cool million.

Bambi watched the power breakfast boys outfitted in their Ralph Lauren polos and Cole-Haan loafers filing in. A particularly bulky member of the group gave her his customary fat-lidded wink and greasy-lipped smile. Bambi sighed into her coffee drink and ordered her fried eggs over easy. *This morning will be a drag,* she thought.

But hold on. The door flung open and in walked Sam Thorne in full regalia—impeccably fitted Armani suit and studied savoir-faire. Bambi knew that Sam wore a suit only when something "BIG" was in the offing. In tow was Guy Tinker, his techno-spook—Silicon Valley's answer to Alger Hiss. Also tagging along, looking keyed up even before sipping a drop of caffeine, was J. W. Neilson, or Doctor Spin as he was called—Vice-President of E-marketing at Thorne's latest venture, Ozzzz.com. *But wait, who's the chick?* wondered Bambi. Hmmm. *Not really his type, though attractive in a preppy kind of way. She can't be more than 22! Okay, Sam's up to his old tricks again!*

Thorne's group sat at a corner table that was farthest away from Bambi's lookout.

You're up to no good, Sam Thorne. Who is this wench? And why have you not replied to my e-mails for the past three days? This better be a good one. Bambi dug into her bag for her cell phone and dialed Sam's cell phone. She could hear it ring on the other side of the restaurant. He picked it up. Before she uttered a word, he inter-cepted, "I'll fill you in tonight at Diavolo's. How about 6:00?"

You think you're so smooth, Sam. Always coming up with the answer before someone can even pose the question. Yeah, all right, I'll meet you in the bar at Diavolo's. I'll be all ears.

"What's it all about, valley? Where's the meaning beyond the cool cars and those cherished plans to tear down the family house and build a mansion?"

Richard Scheinin, San Jose Mercury News Religion and Ethics Writer. Excerpted from the San Jose Mercury News, Wednesday, April 5, 2000 (after the NASDAQ low dip of 634 points, more than twice the previous record of 328 points set a week earlier.)

Chapter 10

Diavolo's Playground

It was 6:30 and Bambi was on her third Martini. Sam was late. Sam was always late. Sam felt that he had a God-given right to be late. It didn't matter, really. Bambi felt like she needed to prime the pump with a few drinks anyway, so his habitual tardiness was a good excuse for a few quiet, meditative moments to alter her brain chemistry.

Diavolo's Forno, venue of dealmakers and deal-breakers, Bambi noticed, was busy, as usual. She recognized a few of the "suits" with graying temples who were clinking glasses with twenty-somethings with visions of IPOs dancing in their heads. Non-disclosure documents were passed around and signed before appetizers were served, and everyone sat hunched over their meals, whispering in low tones and using code names for their projects thwarting eavesdroppers and snoops. Bambi felt a bit wilted. She really wasn't in the mood for backslapping business banter, so she slipped on her Ray-Bans.

She spotted Sam strolling into Diavolo's bar. He was still wearing the Armani suit he had on this morning at Buffalo's. He gave

Bambi a wet kiss full on the lips, sat down next to her, and started sipping her Martini.

"That's *my* drink!" Bambi protested.

"Not anymore." Sam smiled and stroked her nose. "What's on the Digital Diva's mind tonight, hmmm?"

"A couple of Martinis, you loathsome reptile. But never mind that. Let's get down to business. Who's the wench?"

"What wench?"

"You know, the chick you brought into Buffalo's this morning. The one in the Pendletons and starched underwear."

"Oh, you mean Caitlin, my new Director of Web Technology."

"Sam, come off it. What do you take me for, after all these years! I'll bet she thinks Java's something you drink to stay awake at night."

"Actually, Caitlin has quite an impressive pedigree—Ph.D. from MIT in computer science—and, more importantly, a fresh dewy innocence that even *your* plastic surgeon couldn't manufacture. She's perfect for the part."

"And what exactly do you mean, coy-boy?"

"Bambi, don't you see? It's all about image, identity, branding."

"Sam, when are you going to stop believing your own bullshit? You're nothing but a slut in a tie and wingtips."

"I can't believe you don't get it, babe! Caitlin is Dorothy! Ozzzz.com's very own Dorothy! The real thing."

Bambi grabbed Sam's arm. Admittedly, Sam had a genius for marketing and putting just the right spin on things to capture his audience. Smiling, she wagged her finger at him.

"Sam, if I can believe you—and I never know when I can, but I do know you know how to turn a profit and grab marketshare by the ass and never let go—this is almost a stroke of genius. Let me be her image consultant! Do you think we could talk her into wearing braids and ruby slippers? Oh, I'll have a grand time with this one!"

"Bambi, I give you carte blanche in that department. Let me handle the rest."

"The rest of what, exactly?"

"Weeell, you know, the rest—the hype, the PR, the media. That."

"Okay, Sam, you're on, you devious and deviant low-life. I know you like I know myself. So, that said, why don't you come over later. We can have a few cocktails, and ummmm, strategize, if you get my drift."

"My Queen of Silicone, you know I'd love nothing better. Unfortunately, I have a dinner engagement with some media folks tonight. See ya." Sam abruptly stood up and quickly slipped out of the restaurant.

Bambi felt her cheeks flush from too many Martinis. Without a moment's hesitation, she pulled her cell phone out of her handbag and dialed up the cute young Aussie Web developer with a shaved head and nosering who followed her around at last night's product launch party. He was hoping she'd be his angel investor.

"Mickey, darling, it's Bambi, Bambi Rose. About that business plan—come over at 9:30 sharp tonight. I think you have enormous potential."

"The median price of a single-family home in Santa Clara County rocketed through the half-million dollar mark in March, rising nearly 39 percent from the same period a year ago.

The $60,000 jump over February's level is yet another leap in Silicon Valley's unrelenting housing market as cash chases a dwindling supply of houses for sale. The traditionally most active house-buying months of the year are still ahead . . .

Countywide, the median price rose to $539,870 last month—$151,050 higher than the March 1999 figure of $388,820, according to a report released Tuesday by the California Association of Realtors.

Pricey Cities

The top California cities and communities with the highest median home prices in March:

Atherton: $3,350,000

Los Altos Hills: $2,750,000

Monte Sereno: $2,118,000

Hillsborough: $2,000,000

Woodside: $1,500,000"

"Home Prices Through the Roof," by Sue McAllister Mercury News Staff Writer, San Jose Mercury News, Wednesday, April 26, 2000.

Chapter 11

You Can Lead a Horse to Water

Mime-Version: 1.0
Date: Fri, 28 Apr 2000 10:58:16 -0800
To: sailorshanty@safetynet.com
From: Caitlin Leary <cleary@ozzzz.com>
Subject: A place I can call home
Status:

Dear Mom and Dad,

I've spent the past two weeks utterly depressed about the housing situation here. As you know, I need to get out of corporate housing soon and find a more permanent place to live. The rental market here is awful. It's entirely conceivable that a Ph.D. earning a six-figure income could find herself calling a Whole Foods shopping cart "home." Maybe that's why they invented laptops. Yesterday morning, I must have looked at 15 places and did not come up with even one remote possibility. I was under the delusion that $700 or $800 a month could get me some stupendous digs—
a view of the rolling hills, a California garden with lemon trees,

avocado trees, fig trees, a roomy home-office, and a kitchen that even Julia Child would find serviceable.

I'll keep you posted and let you know if I come up with anything. Wish me luck.

Love,
Caitlin

To Caitlin's horror, she discovered that housing under $1,800 per month ranged from monk's quarters to hovels, complete with ripped linoleum floors and 10 years' growth of mold seeping through chipping stucco walls. And the worst part was that everywhere she went, there were dozens of people waiting in line, ready to lay down three or four months rent in advance in cash and even stock options, their eyes aflame with the clear intent to eradicate the competition without remorse. Caitlin felt like she was in a breadline in Mother Russia.

Caitlin decided to take the lid off her budget limit and started looking at higher-priced options.

She found a place on the Web that appeared promising, though more than she wanted to spend. *What the heck,* she thought! *It's worth a look.* The place was advertised as a charming one-bedroom cottage for $3,200 a month in a "pastoral" environment on an estate with horses ten minutes from the freeway in Woodside. It sounded dreamy.

First thing the next morning, Caitlin called for an appointment and headed out. The drive to Woodside was lovely—a windy tree-shaded road that turned into the long driveway to the estate. She pulled up to the sprawling ranch home feeling hopeful and repeating the mantra: *"There's no place like home! There's no place like home!"*

Caitlin rang the doorbell and was greeted by a middle-aged blonde in sweats who reeked of cigarettes. Caitlin was about to step inside but the woman intercepted her.

"Hi, Charlotte Meyerstone." The blonde extended her hand.

Two little girls suddenly appeared at the door, on either side of their mother. Caitlin noticed that they were both wearing the signature Ozzzz.com product—high-heeled red sneakers studded with sequins and jewels.

"I'm Caitlin. Nice to meet you. Well, it looks like your little girls are Ozzzz.com fans. I can spot them a mile away!"

"Yeah, we looooove Ozzzz.com more than anything in the whole wide world," said the older child enthusiastically.

"More than anything! We love Ozzzz.com this much!" chimed in her sister, spreading her arms wide in the air.

"Now, girls. You know that isn't true. You know that you love your parents and your horsies much more than you love Ozzzz.com," Charlotte said.

"Noooooo! Noooooo! Nooooo! We love Ozzzz.com and only Ozzzz.com!" The girls cried out in protest.

"Look, Amanda, Kirsten, Mommy's got business to do, so just stay in the house and play till I finish up. This nice lady may want to live here. And stay off the computers!"

The blonde shooed the girls inside and immediately closed the door behind her, pulling it hard to make sure it was locked. Without much small talk, she led Caitlin to the back of the house to a shaded area where the horse barn stood. A couple of well-toned fillies nodded as the lady of the manor led her up the stairs to the apartment over the barn.

The place was a narrow squeeze with a tiny boxcar of a living room, a windowless bedroom with floorboards that complained vehemently with every step, and a makeshift kitchen consisting of a countertop plug-in double-burner and an office refrigerator. She took Caitlin back out to the porch and pointed out that if she happened to have a lot of clothes, the shed would more than suffice and advised the use of plastic clothing protectors in case of rain. Just then, as a soft California breeze rippled through Caitlin's hair, she was reminded of the downstairs tenants. A waft of fresh hay co-mingled with fresh manure stung her nose.

"Caitlin, this is a steal, let me tell you. You just won't find anything for the price around here. Look at all the natural beauty that surrounds you! And just so you know, we're asking for a minimum of three months' rent in advance. And the highest bidder gets the place. So, if you would fill out this credit app—say, where did you say you worked?"

"Oh, Ozzzz.com actually. I was hired out of MIT to be their Director of Web Technology."

"Why that's terrific. My kids, as you saw, are devout fans! Too devout, if you ask me, but then, they're probably going through some kind of phase. It's a real obsession this Ozzzz.com thing with the kids around here. Frankly, I sometimes get a little worried about them. And you wouldn't believe how the girls have run our credit cards buying all of that Ozzzz.com paraphernalia. I haven't even mentioned it to my husband yet. He'd have a stroke! Anyway, Caitlin, I'm looking for someone just like you, a nice young career girl working for a dotcom. I'm sure you're getting stock options. You know, maybe you could contribute some of your shares to cover the upfront costs. Ozzzz.com's doing very, very well lately."

"Yeah, well, thanks for the opportunity, Mrs. Meyerstone, but I'm not much of an equestrian, I'm afraid. I'm sure someone out there will be eager to snap the place up. Thanks for taking the trouble."

Caitlin watched the lady of the house trot back to her hermetically sealed homestead. Regret, anger, and disgust surged through Caitlin's body. She felt like working-class scum. Walking back to her car, she seriously thought about scoping out a cozy spot under a freeway ramp off Highway 101. At least it would be close to the office.

"I've never looked through a keyhole without finding someone was looking back."

Judy Garland, NBC-TV, March 16, 1967

Chapter 12

New Kid on the Block

Mime-Version: 1.0
Date: Wednesday, 19 Apr 2000 9:58:16 -0800
To: cleary@ozzzz.com
From: $am Thorne <sthorne@ozzzz.com>
Subject: Checking in
Status:

Hi Caitlin,
I thought I'd check in with you to see how Ozzzz.com's been treating you. I trust that you're finding everything agreeable and that you're sufficiently challenged. We have tremendous faith in you and look forward to watching you blossom.

I have a few ideas for the next major site revision that I'd like to run by you. Are you available for a cappuccino offsite around 5:00? I'll meet you at your office.

$am

Twelve times. At least that's how many times she counted, not including periods when she was away from her desk. It seemed like every time she looked up, Sam was walking past her office. Sam Thorne looking reflective, rubbing his chin. Sam Thorne with his suit jacket on. Sam Thorne sans suit jacket with tie loosened slightly at the collar. Sam Thorne deep in discussion with a colleague. Sam Thorne scratching his head distractedly. Sam Thorne striding with determination. *At least he didn't press his nose up against the glass window of her office.* So, in a way, the e-mail was simply the denouement of Sam's serial strolls by her office all day. She knew this was coming after her lunch with Sam, but hoped that he was going to forget. There was no way to wiggle out of this one.

The rest of the day and through her lunch break, Caitlin stayed glued to her desk, laboring diligently on an elaborate strategic plan for upgrading the Ozzzz.com Website for the next major revision, which would be launched by month's end. She wanted to be certain that she had thoroughly prepared the groundwork for their upcoming meeting. Her conscientious nature drove her to prepare a tightly buttoned up plan with every contingency covered. She wondered if Sam was monitoring her every move with the surveillance camera.

By 4:45, Caitlin had two printed copies of her Web strategy plan on her desk, awaiting Sam's review. Fifteen minutes later, Sam appeared (suit jacket on, tie snug) in Caitlin's office.

"Are you ready to go? I thought we'd duck out of Dodge for a little while to free up the energy and meet over at the café around the corner. What's this you've got here?" Sam rifled through Caitlin's plan.

"Oh, nothing much really—just a few ideas for the next rev of the Website—just like you asked." answered Caitlin.

"Oh, we won't need any of that. E-mail me a copy of that tomorrow. I want to hear you out, without notes, without preparation. I want to know what makes Caitlin Leary tick. I want to know what moves you. Is it okay if I get inside your head a little? I'm sure you won't mind?" Sam asked.

Slipping on her jacket, with Sam's assistance, Caitlin flushed slightly, feeling a little foolish for trying to second-guess a brilliant business genius and feeling more than a little nervous again about his attentiveness.

" *...I found myself in the midst of a strange people, who, seeing me come from the clouds, thought I was a great Wizard. Of course I let them think so, because they were afraid of me, and promised to do anything I wished them to.* "

From The Wonderful Wizard of Oz, by Frank Baum, originally published in 1900.

Chapter 13

Single Shot, Wet, A Little Foam

Sam ushered Caitlin into the warm intimacy of the Café Corazón, just around the corner from Ozzzz.com. He led her to a corner table surrounded by a grove of potted plants where they would be shielded from prying eyes.

A young Latino, dressed in black jeans and tee-shirt set off by a black beret and red neckerchief, appeared at the table to take their order.

"I'll take a triple shot of espresso, and for you, Caitlin?" asked Sam, solicitously.

"Oh, just a cappuccino."

"Now, I'm sorry to say, but it's not that simple. You see, here at the Café Corazón, we offer choices, endless choices. So you can have your cappuccino decaf or half-caf, regular, low-fat, non-fat, or soy, a single, a double, a triple, wet, dry. Anyway you want it. Trini—that's me—wants it to be *absolutamente perfecto* for you, *Señorita*!" explained the Latino.

"What do you mean, wet or dry? It's a beverage, so of course it's wet! I just want a plain old cappuccino—caffeinated!" responded Caitlin. Normally she would have been annoyed, but there was something about this guy. *Cute smile and dimples too!*

"Okay, then, a single shot, wet, and a little foam and a triple espresso for the gentleman!"

In less than five minutes, Trini returned with the drinks, giving Caitlin a wink. Caitlin looked up at him and smiled in response.

Sam waved him away, and laid his strong hand on Caitlin's forearm as he spoke.

"Caitlin, I can't tell you how much I appreciate the fact that you've taken me away from that office. I really need to step away from my obsessions sometime, and I rarely allow myself to just sit and have a cup of coffee with a bright young person like you. What a concept—going to a café and just having coffee. I can't express to you what that means to me, Caitlin."

Caitlin tensed up a little, hoping that Sam could not detect her jitters. *What do I say now? God, I feel so lame and hopeless!*

"Well, Mr. Thorne—"

"Remember, it's Sam!" He squeezed her arm warmly, sending chills through her body.

"Sam, yes, of course! This is the land of corporate casual. We're much more formal back East, so please forgive me! What I meant to say was that conversation is very important! My grandfather had a little seaside restaurant in Maine, where I would work summers, and people would come from all over, just for the chowder, the stories, and the conversation. It was so alive!"

"Wait a minute! I know that place. Is it in Rockington Beach, about a stone's throw from the harbor? Great clam chowder served in these huge earthenware bowls?" asked Sam.

"Why, yes! You know it! I can't believe that you were actually there!"

"Yeah, I was visiting my fiancée at Martha's Vineyard at the time, and we had heard about this place. I think it was called the 'Sailor's Shack,' or something along those lines. So we absolutely had to go check it out. We had the time of our lives!"

"The Sailor's Shanty. Was it in the summer? What year? I'll bet I was there, helping Grampa out." *I guess he expects me to remember him, but he probably looked like the other guys in loafers from Wall Street.*

"As a matter of fact, it was during the summer, some years ago, though" replied Sam, draining his triple shot. "And come to think of it, I do remember a sweet long-haired young girl serving bread. That must've been you, Caitlin."

"Yeah, it probably was!" *Shoot! I was just a kid—an Internet virgin! What did I know about Silicon Valley!*

"Caitlin," Sam leaned so close that she could smell the heavy aroma of espresso on his breath, "There are no coincidences.

Do you believe that? I do. I believe that we were destined to be here today to discover this amazing synchronicity. I want to get to know you, Caitlin. There's a lot to you, I can see that, and I see too that you have incredible potential to do extremely well in this Valley. But you've got to want it bad—so bad that it burns your tongue like the hottest salsa you can imagine."

"Mr., er, Sam, I think I do want it. Yes, I really think I do," said Caitlin, feeling herself rapidly slipping away from her center. *I'm supposed to really want "it." Okay, boss, whatever "it" is, I want it.*

"Caitlin. Don't think about it. Tell me you want it, and I'll be there personally to help make it happen for you. I'll promise you that, on my honor. But, there is one thing, that I need from you."

"Oh, sure. Anything you say?" *God, am I being too eager?*

"I want to have coffee with you right here again, on Friday, okay? And then, again, and again. I want to hear your feedback on where Ozzzz.com is going, on where it should be, on how we can help the kids who get on that site everyday become better human beings. Can you give me that?"

"Of course. Friday, after work, sure thing, Mr. Th—er, Sam."

Sam laid a hundred-dollar bill on the table and stood up, pressing her shoulder with his hand. "See you then, Caitlin. Remember what I said." Sam gleamed as he left the café. Tinker had done his usual impeccable job of briefing him on all the pertinent facts. The fact was, clam chowder made Sam gag. He made a mental note to increase Tinker's stock options.

Caitlin slowly rose from the wrought iron chair. Trini came over to the table to retrieve the check and handed Caitlin a red café card coupon, good for one free coffee drink after purchasing five.

"Hey, come back soon, okay? I want to have the pleasure of offering you a free coffee! *Hasta luego!*"

Caitlin left the Café Corazón with a buzz that caffeine alone could not have induced.

*He was a gentleman on whom I built
An absolute trust."*

William Shakespeare, Macbeth

Chapter 14

Mo

Every evening, Mo showed up around 9:00 pm, industrial vacuum cleaner in tow. Mo was the "sanitation engineer" for Ozzzz.com, hand-picked by Sam Thorne, who was in awe of his criminal record and hired him because of it. Though there was no need for it as yet, Sam figured that Mo could perform "preventive maintenance" on anyone who messed with Ozzzz.com's security system. You could have seen Mo kicking butt in an East Oakland street fight. You could have seen Mo getting high with the pipeheads on the corner in Hunter's Point. Or you could have seen Mo serenely divesting a pinstriped investment banker of his cash at gunpoint on Sansome Street. At the same time, he'd have you melting like butter on a biscuit when he captured your gaze with his deep, soulful eyes and crooned 'Summertime' from Gershwin's "Porgy and Bess."

Lately, Mo noticed there was a new face, a very pretty new face, who often stayed around at that hour, which was when the geeks were just warming up for an all-nighter. Caitlin found herself being sucked helplessly into the 80-hour work week vortex and was having a difficult time extracting herself from the routine, often skipping meals, exercise, and sleep to solve one more problem, to make that one additional tweak that would push the Ozzzz.com website to peak performance.

One night, Mo grooved his way into Caitlin's office singing "Georgia on my Mind" and found her head resting on crossed arms on her desk.

"Um, 'scuse me, Miss, but are you, like, all right? I mean, are you feelin' gooooood?"

Not receiving a response, Mo gingerly touched her shoulder.

"Hey, Lady, you dead or alive?"

"Oh!" Caitlin suddenly sat bolt upright, startled out of sleep. "I, I must have dozed off! Yeah, I'm okay, really."

"Well, you look mighty pale to me, Miss. It's beyond just bein' white. I mean sickly pale! Don't you be doin' what those weirdos be doin' here, workin' till the wee hours, sluggin' down the Jolt. You need your beauty sleep, and believe me, you don't look like no geek to me! I betcha you haven't even had your supper tonight!"

"Well, no. I was so busy, I forgot all about it. It's so late! Where would I get anything to eat around here at this hour?" Caitlin asked, still feeling foggy.

"Lemme do you a favor, hon. Look, I got my fifteen minute break comin' up. Lemme walk you over to Trini's place. He's open till midnight. He kinda caters to you Ozzzz.com folks. So let's get you a nice, hot meal, girlie!"

Caitlin grinned. She appreciated Mo's kindness and for a moment, it seemed to her that her Grampa Leary, forever watching over her, had sent Mo out as his goodwill ambassador that night.

"I will gladly accept the invitation from the dashing knight who comes to save the digital damsel in distress!" said Caitlin.

"My innocence begins to wear me down."

Jean Racine, *Andromaque*

Chapter 15

Café Corazón

Caitlin followed Mo to the Café Corazón. She felt her fatigue lift when she saw that Trini was on duty, steaming lattes behind the café's ample glass counter for a motley flock of geeks whom she vaguely recognized, denizens of the Code Closet at Ozzzz.com.

Mo led her to the same table where she had experienced her first one-on-one with Sam. Caitlin shivered slightly as they sat down. *This was weird.* It seemed more than serendipitous to Caitlin that he would choose this particular spot. *It felt like the hotseat.*

"Hey, what's wrong? Should we move to another table?" Mo asked. *My God! Am I that transparent,* Caitlin wondered.

"Oh, no. It's just sort of bizarre that you headed right for this particular table. Sam Thorne and I had a meeting here over coffee just about a week ago. Frankly, I don't even know why I'm so unnerved by it," answered Caitlin, feeling more and more unnerved by Mo at this particular moment.

"I do," Mo's eyes narrowed. "Sam's a dangerous man, and he's snared you into his web. That's what it is. I may look kinda not too smart, but believe me, I been around long enough—on the street and at Ozzzz.com—to know what's up with him. You better watch out for that boy, that's all I gotta say."

"Oh, I think I'm just a little nervous around him." Caitlin tried to flip it off. Why was she in such a state over this? Was Mo trying to scare her, intimidate her for some reason? "He's an incredible power-house of a man. I think I'm simply blown away by the whole thing. To think that he's been taking the time to ask me for opinions!"

"Like I said, you better watch out. I got much more to say on that subject, but before I go on, let's get some food in your belly and mine. Hey, Trini, my man, get this young lady some grub before she keels over. She's been working damn hard. And it's on me!"

Trini dashed to the table offering Caitlin a menu and his wide, warm smile. She immediately felt more at ease. Caitlin noticed that his pants were splashed with big blotches of colorful paint.

"Hey, Señorita, I remember you! You were in here the other day with Sam Thorne! This is on the house! How about some nice homemade chile relleno?" offered Trini. "Oh, and excuse my appearance today. I was painting murals all morning with the kids down in East San Jose, and I didn't have time to change."

"Well, all right, I guess so. I haven't had a whole lot of Mexican food that didn't make me downright queasy," said Caitlin. In Maine, South-of-the-Border translated to Boston-baked beans drowning in Tabasco, something that she generally avoided. *Well, he's Mexican, so maybe it'll be edible.* "But, look, I'm sure that if you're preparing it, whatever it is will be delicious."

In short order, two huge platters of stuffed green chilies smothered with cheese accompanied by mounds of rice and beans landed in front of Caitlin and Mo. Trini pulled up a chair and joined them.

Caitlin tasted a mouthful of the dish in front of her. It was surprisingly good. *Trini you're scoring points without even trying!*

"So, Mo, I want to hear more about Sam. What did you mean when you said that he was dangerous? I want to know everything about him," asked Caitlin. Suddenly it hit her that here she was sharing food with two street-smart guys, so very different from herself, whom she guessed probably never even surfed the 'Net once in their lives and most likely could care less.

"Yeah, well, as my man, Trini, can tell you. You're not the first lovely young thing Sam's sniffed out. You see, women are Sam's recreational drug, you might say. And for him, part of the excitement is all of the corporate foreplay. I suppose he took you out for one of his sincere heart-to-heart 'business meetings' already. I'm tellin' you, girl, watch out," warned Mo, wagging his finger at her.

"Oh, come on, I can't buy that!" protested Caitlin. *Then again, come to think of it, this isn't the first time I've heard this. That man on the plane said the same thing about Sam.*

"Well, *Señorita*, I can tell you he was like a hungry jaguar in the jungle with you the other day when you two came here for coffee. I've seen it all before, and I don't particularly like it. But, there's not too much I can say about it. He leaves huge tips, and keeps us alive," said Trini, squeezing her forearm.

"Yeah, and it's not just a piece of you-know-what—excuse the expression—that he's after, Miss. Sometimes he has these meetings with the big boys late into the night, and oh man, the things that are said in the hallowed halls of Ozzzz.com would make your toes curl," continued Mo.

"That doesn't seem right! The company seems to be riding on such an incredibly wonderful, pure vision. How could he be driven by anything but positive motives? Hey, you're both great guys, but personally, I think Sam's an absolutely brilliant and compelling man," said Caitlin.

"Don't be fooled by his ways. Mo knows what he's talking about. We've heard stories about some of his casualties, and it's not a pretty picture. So, just don't let him drag you down. You're a charming woman, Caitlin, and you deserve so much better!" said Trini. Caitlin felt herself being gently cradled in his caring gaze. It felt like a safe place. And she remembered that she hadn't really experienced that feeling since she left her home in Maine.

"Okay. Okay. So maybe he's a ladies' man, but what about these meetings he has with the big boys, Mo? What are you trying to tell me?" Caitlin fidgeted, exasperated with Mo for not telling her more.

"Miss, one day, when you're ready to hear it, I'll be ready to tell it. Believe me, Ozzzz.com's no fairy tale. Look, I gotta get back to work. They're payin' me to do my job, so I better get my rear in gear and earn my keep. Trini, be sure to take good care of this babe, here. Catch you later."

"But, you see, the Land of Oz has never been civilized, for we are cut off from all the rest of the world. Therefore, we still have witches and wizards amongst us.

From The Wonderful Wizard of Oz, by Frank Baum, originally published in 1900.

Chapter 16

The Coven

Every month, on the full moon, Bambi hosted her women's circle. She allowed nothing to get in the way of this gathering. Absolutely nothing. Not even an IPO.

Bambi inspected the elaborate buffet table that Luz, her live-in, had prepared. Luz knew exactly how to please her mistress. She learned early that by studying Martha Stewart for aesthetics and Alice Bailey for knowledge of the occult, she could create an ambience that would set an appropriate tone for the evening's festivities. Sometimes, Luz would play her own secret jokes on her mistress's friends. Often, she would tuck into the centerpiece arrangement a charm given to her by her Mexican grandmother (the village curandera) and mumble old spells that her abuelita had taught her as a child while she casually sang inane lovesongs in Spanish as she prepared for the fête. Bambi thought that all of this was just an ethnic eccentricity and found it "cute."

The ladies made their entrances. There was much pecking of powdered cheeks and fussing about appearances and outfits.

In a flowing purple goddess gown of beaded silk with spangled earrings that brushed her shoulders, Bambi appeared at the front door and waved her sisters on into the sacred space. The room reeked of sandalwood and myrrh incense. Clusters of candles nervously flamed their fiery spires, creating shadowy phantasms. Surround sound amplified by Dolby reverberated the basso profundo of ominous Druid chanting.

The women arranged themselves around the room, striking poses on the tasseled velvet floor pillows and on the brocade chaise lounges that flanked a circle of crystals and other treasures and artifacts unearthed from wisewoman.com. Each of the participants had a "totem," a mouthpiece through which she could feel comfortable speaking her uncensored truth in the presence of her sisters. The procedure was for the women to put their totems into the center of the room. Whenever someone had something to reveal, she would retrieve her totem and stand in the center of the room and speak to the group without interruption for five minutes until Bambi sounded a large Tibetan gong.

As Bambi helped Luz pour fulsome goblets of rich Merlot, the women placed their totems in the center of the circle. The women had decided that Beanie Babies would serve as the best totems, since there was a wide selection to choose from and they would quickly become valuable collector's items on eBay. Bambi sent rounds of wine to the circle followed by plump, neatly rolled joints and platefuls of artful hors d'oeuvres. As libations and inhalations swirled around the room, formalities, niceties, and pretensions dropped away. The women hunkered down and let loose.

Jaqui Childers let out a whoop and jumped into the circle, clutching her black cat Beanie Baby, "Eartha Kitty," to her bosom. She flicked back her black bangs from her forehead and, placing her fist on her hip, struck a decidedly Cher-like pose. (She had studied Cher's surgical alterations over the years in order to make sure that her own cosmetic surgeon did not a miss single tuck or furrow.) "I don't know how to say this tactfully, but here goes! Maddy Longman (she pointed the stuffed animal at a sallow, puffy-eyed blonde in turquoise)—your husband is a total slimeball. Do you know that at the last Woodside Elementary School auction he had the nerve to ask me if 'it was all real, or was it Memorex' as he was groping me in the backseat of your gold beemer! That man not only suffers from bad taste, he can't even—" The gong reverberated deeply.

Maddy staggered up to the circle and gripped her froggie Beanie Baby tightly at the throat.

"I would like to speak my truth." Maddy started wailing inconsolably, and another sister, Joanie Ferre, scooped up her elephant Beanie Baby, her bottom jiggling, as she scurried to the rescue. Leaning into Joanie's billowy body, Maddy cried out, "He's not a slimeball. He's a scumbag. He's rat poison. He's an earthworm. He's driven me to drink! There's only one person who's a bigger louse than my husband—and that's Sam Thorne!"

At the mention of Sam's name, all of the women jumped up, thrashing pillows around the room, smashing wine glasses into the sacred circle, and unleashing fearsome squeals of disgust punctuated by supplications and prayers: "Annihilate him!" "Sam the scam!" "String him up by his balls!" "Chop it off!" "Incubus. Succubus. Kill the cowardly, lowlife cuss!" "Slam bam, thank-you, mam. Now it's your turn, Sam!"

In the shadows, Luz shook her head and smirked. "Abuelita, muchas gracias! This is much funnier than the videos! These rich white people are so foolish!"

Bambi struck the gong with vehement ferocity. She took her place in the circle. This happened only under extremely rare and significant circumstances. The women settled down and sucked in their breath.

Gently stroking her Gila monster Beanie Baby, Bambi spoke. "All of us have suffered from the exploitation of Sam Thorne. How many of you have suffered through the 60-second manager's approach to sexual pleasure, the God-awful fantasies, the rejections, the lies, the betrayals, and what about the pain and embarrassment of the diseases and the abortions! What about all that, Jaqui? Joanie, would you be such a blimp today if it hadn't been for Sam? And Maddy, do you think for a second it was your husband that turned you into an alcoholic? Remember Sam's baby? And the rest of you. Look at you, all of you, the pathetic victims of the soul-less scourge of Silicon Valley. I want to help you move beyond your victim mentality. I want to help you become the women you were born to be. I want to offer you this sacred ground as a place where you can all become as powerful as me!"

"Her eyes closed in spite of herself and she forgot where she was and fell among the poppies, fast asleep."

From The Wonderful Wizard of Oz, by Frank Baum, originally published in 1900.

Chapter 17

In the Wizard's Chambers

Mime-Version: 1.0
Date: Friday, 21 Apr 2000 10:16:16 -0800
To: cleary@ozzzz.com
From: $am Thorne <sthorne@ozzzz.com>
Subject: Touchbase
Status:

Hi Caitlin,
I just wanted to thank you for sharing your insights with me the other night! I really enjoy that kind of stimulating give-and-take. I'd like to discuss some ideas I've been kicking around about the Web promotion of our launch event in May. I'll see you in my office at 5:30.

$am

Another e-mail from Sam. After her encounter with Mo and his cryptic warnings, Caitlin felt a tad edgy, but quickly brushed away her doubts. *What does an old janitor like Mo know anyway!* There was probably no cause for concern. Maybe Mo was envious, or it could have been that Mo viewed Sam as the oppressor and had a knee-jerk reaction to him as he would toward any successful and powerful white man. *I'm not going let Mo get me down.* She actually looked forward to the second meeting, and even more so knowing that Sam didn't expect her to come up with a brilliant marketing plan in less than 24 hours.

Caitlin temporarily shelved her thoughts about that evening's meeting and immersed herself in her work. With the next revision of the Ozzzz.com site due in less than two weeks, there was a long list of to-do items to sink her teeth into.

At about 12:30, Caitlin received a call from the front desk.

"Caitlin, your lunch has arrived," announced the receptionist.

"Lunch? But I didn't order anything."

"Well, it's got your name on it, and there's a latte here for you, too."

"Can you have someone bring it to my office? I'm in the middle of something critical at the moment." Caitlin wondered what the heck was going on.

The receptionist appeared with a brown paper bag imprinted with red hearts and an 18-ounce plastic commute mug with a spill-proof top. Caitlin thanked her and opened the bag, which was warm to the touch. She pulled out a Styrofoam to-go container. On the lid was taped a small envelope. Caitlin opened the envelope and pulled out a hand-painted note decorated with Spanish graffiti. She grinned, shaking her head. Of course! This was Trini's doing! *Para mi princesa! Buen provecho! From Trini! And next time I see you, I will make sure that I am not covered with paint!*

Fortified by Trini's attention and his scrumptious turkey sandwich, Caitlin had her most productive afternoon ever since landing at Ozzzz.com. Project schedules were set, resources allocated, and tasks delegated. It gave her a sense of satisfaction knowing that the machine—the Ozzzz.com website—would have every bolt tightened and would be ready to roll out of the showroom on time.

5:00, then 5:15, then 5:30 rolled around, and her memory jolted her into the present. Sam was waiting for her! Caitlin sped down the hall to his office and knocked on the door. Sam opened the door, clutching his Palm Pilot. He gave it a quick glance, punched a button, and motioned for Caitlin to sit down. Caitlin took her position on one end of a lime green suede neo-Italian sofa that must have been at least eight feet long. It was supported by ultra-thin, tapered chrome legs that ended in almost stiletto-like points, and Caitlin marveled at the design engineering, which kept it from tipping or collapsing.

"Just checking on the NASDAQ. It's sort of an obsession with me, so please don't think that I'm ignoring you, Caitlin. Hey, before we start, why don't we have a cocktail? Or, coffee? Whatever you like. I think I'll fix myself a Martini. Pick your poison."

"Oh, let me think for a moment," Caitlin replied, wondering if this was a test. *I hate martinis! Ok, be grown up about this. Have a cocktail with him, or he'll think you're some innocent lightweight and lose all respect for you.* "Yes. That's sounds like just the thing. I'll have the same. Oh, and make it a double!"

Sam walked over to a sleek mahogany armoire and opened the cabinet doors, revealing a full bar stocked with colorful hand-blown crystal decanters and glasses for every occasion that sparkled like jewels against the mirrored interior. He pulled out two gold-flecked martini glasses from the small built-in refrigerator and proceeded to mix the drinks.

"A double, huh? Well, you must've had a tough day! Or maybe you're just a bit of a party girl?"

Sam handed Caitlin a frosty martini glass with a red-eyed olive submerged in the double shots of gin and vermouth.

"Here's to our brilliant future!" Caitlin clinked her glass against Sam's and gulped down a full sip, feeling her throat and chest burn. *This stuff is awful! I'll have to drink it down really fast.* She could have sworn that the olive winked at her.

"Caitlin, I'd like to show you something I've been working on. Stand in front of the bookcase, if you please."

Caitlin did Sam's bidding, slugging down her martini and feeling a hot, heady rush thundering through her temples. It felt as if the floor was moving! *Get a grip! You are such a cheap drunk!*

In less than a nanosecond, Caitlin found herself in a darkened room with no corners. In the center of the room was a round cushion that looked like a giant marshmallow. She lowered herself into the cushion steadying herself with her palms on the plush fabric. The room suddenly brightened and spun around her slowly, hypnotically. A tropical panorama flashed onto the wrap-around walls, enveloping her senses. Frothy blue waves washing over the white sands. Palms swaying in the soft warm wind. In fact, Caitlin could even feel the soft wind and ocean spray on her skin. There was a fragrance of some sort too, a deliciously intoxicating floral aroma that Caitlin found irresistible. She took a few deep breaths, gradually feeling herself merge with her environment, feeling her boundaries subtly dissolving until she was one with the ambience.

Caitlin felt Sam's body leaning into hers and his warm breath on her ears.

"So what do you think of my universe? I'll bet you never thought you'd end up in a tropical paradise when you woke up this morning. This is just a prototype of my hyper-reality model, a completely virtual sensory experience, perceived to be so real by the human nervous system that it's almost impossible to distinguish it from the genuine article. It's actually even better than the real thing. We've added a few algorithms that simulate the alpha state to hyper-react, so you receive an even more heightened experience," whispered Sam. "So what do you think, Caitlin?"

Caitlin strained to make sense of what he was saying. *This is impossibly beautiful.* Her attention was riveted on the scene in front of her, and Sam's hard male body pressing against her left side, his breath on the back of her neck. For only a fleeting moment, she felt herself looking for the switch that would flip her mental awareness on again, but sensation overrode logic, understanding, and reason. *This feels so extraordinary. I've never been in this place before. I've never felt so free and at ease!*

Above her, a macaw swooped out of a coconut tree, a splash of red and green feathers against the cloudless blue sky. Suddenly, Caitlin felt the cool silk of her blouse sliding down her skin and her bare shoulder melting into Sam's broad palm. Enveloped by the balmy sea breeze and the sweet scent of frangipani, she surrendered her lips to his and felt her body receding into Sam's like the sand being washed into the ocean by soft, unrelenting waves.

"Caitlin. Ahhhh. Caitlin…"

"He is a good Wizard. Whether he is a good man or not, I cannot tell, for I have never seen him."

From The Wonderful Wizard of Oz, by Frank Baum, originally published in 1900.

Chapter 18

Virtual Home

Oh my God, what have I done! Well, what have I done?
Caitlin dragged herself back to her corporate apartment with its rented furnishings.

Tea. Hot tea and bed. That always helps. Good for whatever ails you, as Mom always said. God, Mom, I wish you were here right now!

Caitlin comforted herself with some herbal tea and sighed herself into bed, pulling the quilt up to her chin. Tonight's encounter with Sam yanked her down into a state of consciousness she had never experienced before. She wasn't sure if she was intrigued or disgusted. What was it about that man that captivated her like that? Whatever it was, it made her vastly uneasy. She felt like something indefinably sinister was at work here, but she had no idea what it could be. On the surface, the incident was nothing but an interlude—granted under very strange circumstances—but objectively, only that. Still, there was a knowing that she carried about the incident that she couldn't yet verbalize.

Caitlin wished that she had an addictive personality so that she could put it out of her mind with some drug of choice. In fact, she hardly indulged in anything stronger than an occasional beer or glass of wine with dinner—and martinis lately. Besides, there was nothing in the house.

So, she took a deep breath and called in the spirit of Grandpa Leary, who always seemed to be there for her whenever her life took a rocky turn. Half awake and half-asleep, she heard her name being called out. It was Grampa Leary. There was a smile in his voice, the same smile she recalled as a child. She felt her forehead suddenly get cool and her grandfather's comforting hand softly rubbing away her cares and she sunk into a deep sleep.

Caitlin drifted into a reverie about the home she had left behind. She felt the sting of the salty sea air on her cheeks and the damp wind waving through her hair. Often, as a teenager, she would take long walks along Rockington Beach with Grampa after they had closed up the "Sailor's Shanty" for the night. Caitlin loved working in her grandfather's restaurant. Five bucks would get you a hunk of homemade Irish soda bread, the best clam chowder on the Eastern seaboard, and a pint of stout.

The Sailor's Shanty was a legendary place. In the summers, it drew tourists who came up from Martha's Vineyard just to savor the chowder and Grampa Leary's colorful storytelling. It was a place where pretension couldn't survive. Six-figure New York financiers and lobster fishermen sat elbow to elbow at the long wooden communal tables slurping beers and sharing the humor and joy that Grampa Leary generated. And in the winter, when things were quieter, it was usually the locals who came out to sit in the warmth of the fireplace and in the convivial company of friends.

Caitlin saw herself walk into The Sailor's Shanty on just such a night, looking for her grandfather. A couple of old salts—Jeremy Hallihan and Trevor Flynn—waved her to their table.

"Caitlin, look at ye! Ye're a regular business lady, y'are, all serious-like. Ye haven't fergotten yer old friends, have ye?" said Trevor, puffing on his hand-carved pipe.

Caitlin gave each of the men a peck on their stubbly cheeks.

"No, of course not! But, I'll tell you, since I've been in California, I seemed to have forgotten myself. Hey, have you seen my Grampa anywhere?"

"Why, no, Caitlin, haven't ye heard?" asked Jeremy

"Heard what?"

"Well, he took off about a week ago, it was. Said he was goin' out to look for ye. Said he heard ye were lost."

Caitlin sank into the bench next to Jeremy and buried her head in his damp wool overcoat, her entire body heaving with sorrow.

"Bewitched, Bothered, and Bewildered"

Lorenz Hart, Song Title, Pal Joey, 1940.

Chapter 19

Ghosts

"Caitlin, you look like you've just seen a ghost!"

"That's no joke, Trini!" Caitlin collapsed into the first available chair at the Café Corazón. After the confusing interlude with Sam followed by the dream about her grandfather, Caitlin couldn't bear to drag herself to the office. The prospect of running into Sam at the office and having to act nonchalant seemed like a Herculean endeavor. Instead, she rolled out of bed feeling numb and headachy and stumbled unceremoniously into the Café Corazón, in running shorts and a sweatshirt, her hair loose and wild. Instinct drove her to a safe haven, where she could wobble around in her foggy state without feeling judged and without having any demands placed on her.

Trini tore around the counter and sat down at the table with Caitlin, taking her cold hands in his.

"What in the world is going on with you? How come you're not at work? Something's not right. Tell me. No, I take that back, you don't have to tell me anything. Just stay right there. I'll whip up some eggs and coffee for you."

Trini, you are the saint of Silicon Valley! You truly are! Caitlin, as always, appreciated his nurturing attentiveness and the fact that he just let her be. She really couldn't get her arms around what had happened over the past 24 hours, and was relieved to just be with the perplexing melange of emotions swirling inside her. She was not ready to even attempt to make sense of anything just yet. So odd too that she made a beeline to the café, as if she was on automatic pilot. Someone or something else was definitely at the helm this morning.

Trini returned with her breakfast and topped off the presentation with a single rose, white with frilly pink edges, in a green and purple raku bud vase in the shape of a mermaid.

"Trini, you never cease to amaze me! Everything you do is so artful, down to the way you swirl foam into a little peak in my lattes. And this vase! She's gorgeous!"

"I want you to take her home with you. In fact, she is you. I created her in your image. Didn't you grow up near the ocean?"

"Yes, in Maine, on the Atlantic. Did I tell you that? I don't remember. In fact, today I can barely remember my own name or how I got here. Do you ever have days like that?"

"Well, to be honest, no. Maybe you've been working too hard, or spending too much time on the Internet. Or is it something else?"

Caitlin looked down at the two fried eggs on her plate. She poked her fork into the yolks. Their yellow tears slowly dribbled over the translucent whites.

"Um, yeah. It's something else. I'm not going in to work today. You've probably figured that out by looking at me. I feel like an utter rag."

"No! You're beautiful, just a little distraught, a little upset. Listen, if you want to tell me, I am here to listen and support you, always. I mean it. I don't own a cell phone, I don't own a pager, and I don't own a computer, but my heart tells me everything I need to know. This morning before you showed up, I was setting up the bakery counter, and I was suddenly filled with a sense of intense distress. Something was very wrong, but I couldn't put my finger on it. I examined the way things were going with me, and I realized that this sense of panic had nothing to do with me, but with someone close to me. So when you walked in like this, all upset and full of pain, I knew you were calling on me for support. I heard you with my heart...much more reliable than a cell phone!"

"You did? Really, Trini, the last thing I want to do is trouble you with my issues! You've been too, too kind...sending over the lunches to the office, and always finding time to say 'Hello' when I come around. Really, I only came here because...well, because, I didn't know where else to go. I had this dream about my grandfather, and he was looking all over for me, but couldn't find me. He said I was lost!" Caitlin unleashed a gush of tears, feeling foolish for not knowing what she was crying about. Grampa Leary was right...she *was* lost.

"Oh, *Preciosa*! You're like a little flower that's just experienced her first terrible thunderstorm!" Trini cocooned Caitlin in his protective arms. She felt soothed by his tenderness, which she welcomed at this moment.

"Trini, something really weird happened last night. It wasn't just the dream about my grandfather…It happened at the office… with, uh, with…"

"Let me guess, Sam Thorne!"

"Wait, what did *he* tell you?"

"We're not exactly bosom buddies, Caitlin! He didn't have to tell me anything! You wore it all over your face like a billboard the minute you walked in. I told you before, Sam's relentless. At least he has good taste, I'll give him that. Are you okay? Did he hurt you, Caitlin?"

"Oh, God, Trini, I feel so confused and wasted. Yes, we were… together. No, he didn't hurt me, not physically. But I know that somehow I'm different. I feel so spaced out, like my will has been sapped. I don't feel like myself at all. There's something seriously wrong. I feel like I'm under his spell, and believe me, I don't go for that type of vacuous New Age thinking. Maybe I'm just over-worked and suffering from a bad case of homesickness."

"This isn't sounding too good. It doesn't fit the profile."

"Profile? What do you mean by that?"

"Believe me, I've seen many of Sam's victims come through this place, most of them pretty angry at that guy for overstepping boundaries. At first, they acted just like you, kind of smitten with his power and charm, but once they experienced the real Sam Thorne, most of them got pretty bent out of shape. You don't seem, angry, though. Somehow, he's affected you in a very different way. It makes me wonder about his agenda with you. Caitlin, listen, it sounds like you have a lot of sorting out to do. Do me a favor. Go home and relax, take a nap, read, watch a video…just hang, okay? I'm going to call you around 2:00, after the lunch rush is over, to check in. If you're up for it, I would be honored to take you out sometime. No pressure, okay? We can talk more about it when you're feeling up to it. "

"Trini, I feel like such a wreck! You're absolutely right, I do need to rest. I don't feel exactly angry with Sam, no reason to get angry with him, really. On the other hand, I feel terribly out of sorts. Anyway, Trini, thanks again, for everything. You've been so kind to me. I'll wait for your call. I will." Caitlin hugged Trini warmly and walked out into the bright California sun, buoyed up—at least for the moment—by Trini's genuine concern, but still deeply unsettled by the events that had transpired over the past 12 hours.

"Nothing in earlier history matches this corporate group's power to penetrate the social landscape. Using both old and new technology, by owning each other's shares, engaging in joint ventures as partners, and other forms of cooperation, this handful of giants has created what is, in effect, a communications carrier...At issue is not just a financial statistic, like production numbers or ordinary industrial products like refrigerators or clothing. At issue is the possession of power to surround almost every man, woman, and child...with controlled images and words, to socialize each new generation of Americans, to alter the political agenda of the country. And with that power comes the ability to exert influence that in many ways is greater than that of schools, religion, parents, and even government itself."

Ben Bagdikian, *The Media Monopoly*

Chapter 20

Branded

"Okay, guys, I need your help. Bad. Real bad. This is major. Thorne's all over my ass about coming up with 'the Thing' about Ozzzz.com. It's gotta be the genuine article. It's gotta sing to the Webrats out there. It's gotta have finesse. And it's gotta be on Thorne's desktop by end of day. So, c'mon, show me whatcha got."

J.W. Neilsen paced across the expanse of the main conference of Ozzzz.com also known as "Kansas," burning a trail into the carpet during the first 15 minutes of the meeting. When J.W. spoke, the room jittered. No matter where you sat in the room, you felt as if you were being pelted with sweat bullets emanating from his jerky frame. Neilsen had the crazed lean and hungry look of a marathon runner, marathon caffeine consumer and marathon marketeer. His knowledge bank was an exhaustive collection of brands, logos, taglines, ads, labels, and media images, which informed his every emotion, his every opinion, and his every motivation.

Today, he had assembled a mandatory meeting of anyone who'd ever had a creative thought at Ozzzz.com—swarms of Web content creators, game producers, product managers, designers, baby marketing geniuses, and, of course, Caitlin. Everyone busied himself or herself scarfing down bagels and cappuccinos, hoping that they wouldn't be singled out and asked to participate in J.W.'s desperate brainstorming.

"Okay. We're talkin' something that sets Ozzzz.com apart, something that worms its way into those tiny young consumer minds and turns them into Ozzzz-aholics. We're talkin' addiction, keeping 'em glued to our site. I'm lookin' for something that makes them think differently. Hold on. Think differently. That's it!" J.W.'s carotid arteries throbbed like a beating drum as he sopped up a dripping brow.

A diffident hand went up.

"Uh, J.W., I believe there's already been a twist on that one…I think we're talking potential copyright violations," piped up a young alpha female in wire-rimmed glasses and the face of a Botticelli cherub.

J.W. sniggered and swatted her remark to a far corner of the room as if he were throwing a curve ball.

"Yeah, yeah, yeah. I know. I know. I was just tryin' to see if you guys were still with me. Okay, so stay with me, would ya? That's good. Now let's try something. You're gonna think I'm a freak, but I don't care. Let's get the juices flowin.' I want you to think of things that you like, things that are important to you in life. Okay. Okay. Here are examples. What do I like? I like Movado watches, Skechers sneakers, Godiva chocolates, online trading, Costa Rican coffee. Get it? Clean. Essential. Elegant. Raj, Viki, anyone, give me some goddam concepts!"

Silence, then a few dribbles . . ..

"Doctor Marten shoes."
"LaserTag."
"Palm computing."
"Online dating."
"Dry martinis with olives."
"Boxer shorts"

"Okay. Okay. You're grasping. That's good. We're just loosening up some gray matter. Caitlin, what about you?"

"Well, how about foghorns in the night or clam chowder with homemade Irish soda bread or the smell of the churning ocean during a storm?" Caitlin offered.

"What've you been reading lately, Moby Dick? We're talking about brand identity, not Captain Ahab. We're reaching out to touch into the underbelly of cyber marketing. Ozzzz.com needs a hook. We need a …"

With an emphatic swoosh, the conference room door flung open as if propelled by a capricious gust of wind. "Personality!" announced Bambi Rose, as she strode across the room in riding boots, brandishing a horse switch. As if clinging for support in a tempestuous windstorm, J.W. found himself plastered up against the whiteboard drenched in the downpour of his own sweat.

"Brilliant," he gasped feebly.

"Yes! A brilliant personality," affirmed Bambi, cracking the switch against the wall inches away from J.W.'s quaking flesh. "Ozzzz.com is screaming out for someone who can act as a role model for these children. Someone dazzling and sublime at the same time. Someone charismatic yet convincing and genuine," continued Bambi, ignoring J.W.

The conference attendees rolled their eyes unanimously.

"After several closed-door sessions all week, Sam and I have come up with a concept. Look guys, I need your help with the implementation. We have exactly two weeks to get this project off the ground, so we need an all-out team effort. By tomorrow, all of you will receive a plan and milestones from J.W. Right now, I need to meet with Raj, Viki, Caitlin, and J.W. The rest of you, take the afternoon off…it's the calm before the storm, so enjoy the rest of your day."

After much shoulder shrugging and quizzical tittering, the room cleared out except for the chosen ones, who clustered around Bambi at one end of the immense mirror-topped conference table.

Bambi silently etched spirals into the surface of the table with her fingertip, appearing utterly lost in her Zen-like pursuit. She had picked up this trick from an ex-Tibetan monk turned networking entrepreneur. It was a way of centering herself and hypnotizing everyone present with her odd repetitive behavior before tossing the Molotov cocktail into the crowd. In a low, soft voice, she laid out her scheme.

"How many of us as children yearned for a special friend? That someone whom you admired and adored, and who knew all of your little secrets. And somehow, even your best friend couldn't quite live up to the standard. So what did you do? You created your own imaginary friends, or borrowed them from books or television. And in your minds, you could always have a little chat with that special friend no matter where you were or what you were doing. Sam and I want to give our community of Ozzzz.com kids just such a friend, right on line, so that whenever they log in, they can look forward to a kind, friendly presence and look up to that person as a guide and teacher. We are going to create Ozzzz.com's own 'Virtual Dorothy.'"

Everyone nodded solemnly, including Caitlin, though she herself never personally felt compelled to create any kind of imaginary buddies, as her real friends and family—especially her grandfather more than adequately filled the bill.

Bambi revved up the volume.

"J.W., I want you to put together an action plan and schedule and distribute it to our Creative Department ASAP. Raj and Viki, you'll be the tag team for rolling out the PR and ad campaign, including the launch party and live Web broadcast. And Caitlin..." Bambi paused, segueing into a handshake, "Well, Caitlin, congratulations. You've just been branded."

"It's vulgar to be famous.

That isn't what makes you great."

Boris Pasternak, The Tragic Years

Chapter 21

Virtual Makeover

"Now, everyone, close your eyes! You'll never guess what I snatched up on eBay!"

The hive of marketeers and make-up artists fussing and flitting around Caitlin froze mid-flutter, eyelids firmly glued together at Bambi's command. Caitlin disobeyed, instead, sitting bolt upright in her chair, craning her neck to see over the crowd in front of her. *My God! I don't believe her. Those must've cost a small fortune! Enough to pay off my parents' mortgage, at least!*

"Okay! Now open your eyes!"

With her arms raised over her head, Bambi clacked out a flamenco-like rhythm with two glitter-encrusted red shoes that she wore over her hands like mittens.

"Judy's ruby reds for our own Virtual Dorothy. Now give me your feet, hon. Let's see how they look on you." Caitlin looked down at her size 8 feet. Ms. Garland's red slippers looked like they were made for a Munchkin. Size 5 and a half, at the most. Judy was probably barely pubescent when she made that movie. Bambi bent over and jammed Caitlin's feet into the ruby slippers.

"That's hot! Now stand up."

Caitlin winced. Gripping the arms of her chair, she pushed herself to a standing position. She felt like a Chinese courtesan wobbling on stubby, painful bound feet.

"Let's take some shots of just her feet, walking, skipping, running a little...and put some playfulness into it, Caitlin!"

At Bambi's recommendation, the cameraman who had been taking close-ups of Caitlin all morning—with pigtails, with hair down, laughing, grinning, shouting with joy—instantly dropped down to the floor on his belly, aiming the camcorder at Caitlin's feet. Caitlin hopped around, nearly turning her ankle, and gracefully (she thought) recovering, skipped down the length of her office, her face twisted in racking pain. Good thing they didn't expect her to force a smile through all of this.

"Bambi, really I don't think I can do this much longer. I really need to take these things—"

"—And prop them up on my lap!" chimed in Sam, who unexpectedly burst into the room, his level, laser gaze zeroing in on Caitlin and Caitlin alone.

"Here, take a load off," Sam slid a chair under Caitlin, who was grateful for small favors. "I'll sit next to you, and you can cross your feet right here on my lap."

Caitlin felt herself being consumed by Sam's gaze, and she momentarily found herself spacing out, oblivious to the frenetic sounds and movements around her. *Oh, my God, It's happening again. What's coming over me?*

As Sam hoisted her legs up onto his lap, gently arranging them, left over right, for the most ideal camera angle, she felt a subtle wave of electricity shoot through the length of her body.

The cameraman, Caitlin suddenly noticed, was now kneeling in front of them, his apparatus stuck to his face, like an appendage he was born with. Caitlin wondered if the poor man chose this calling because he was painfully shy or perhaps had pockmarks from a merciless bout of adolescent acne.

It seemed like she had her feet on Sam's lap for an inordinately long time, and imagined that everyone in the room was clucking their tongues and giving one another the old wink-wink.

"Okay, let's take a break. Great session. Just fabulous!" said Bambi, dismissing the entourage. "Whatever you two have in mind now is none of my affair, but, if you'll pardon me, I would like to have my ruby red slippers back. Now!"

Bambi held out both hands while Sam pried the shoes off of Caitlin's swollen feet and plopped them unceremoniously in Bambi's open hands. What relief! And what unbelievable pain! Quarter-sized blisters pulsed on her big toes and heels. She felt drained and pathetic. A Ph.D. in computer science trotting around in front of a camera like a tortured show dog! This is not what I had in mind at all! What have I turned into! A cheap canine act doing tricks on demand! I am so mortified!

Bambi left the room, slamming the door behind her. Alone again with Sam for the first time since their virtual reality rendezvous, Caitlin felt frail and vulnerable. He could have done anything to her at this moment. If he had taken her in his arms at that very moment, she would have crumbled into dust like a piece of parchment. Whatever name you would attach to Caitlin's response to Sam, one thing was certain, she had no will to push back or challenge anything Sam could do or say to her.

"Caitlin, you are Dorothy. There is no doubt of that to me. You were so beautiful in those slippers. Perfection. I am so touched that you would do this for me, for my creation, for our creation. I just want to thank you from the bottom of my heart." Sam lifted her hand with his fingertips, as it he were holding a butterfly and brushed his lips over the back of her hand. And then he disappeared.

Caitlin looked down at her feet, as if apologizing to them for subjecting them to the brutal scourge of the ruby slippers. A tear splashed down, washing over the flaming blister on her right toe.

"Prophet rules!"

Sam Thorne, CEO of Prophet Corporation and Ozzzz.com

Chapter 22

Coup de Grace

Sam leaned over to Mo who was standing by the bar in Sam's office and whispered some instructions as Avi Ben-Hura and Bob Portell staked out their positions. *This is going to be sweet,* thought Sam. *Activate audio and video.* Mo reached into a cupboard filled with all varieties of drink mixes and pushed a tiny green button on a control panel the size of a business card discreetly mounted in the back of the cupboard.

"Gentlemen, welcome. Make yourselves at home. Mo, over here, has been cleared for security. No worries there. Mo's my man, aren't you, bro'?" Sam smiled at Mo and all but winked.

"I am unconditionally your man, Sir!" affirmed Mo.

"Mo, how about fixing the gentlemen some refreshments? Avi, the usual double vodka with a splash of cranberry, and Bob, a very White Russian for you?"

Avi and Bob nodded. While Mo busied himself at the bar, Sam grabbed a chair and turned it around, straddling it cowboy-style.

"I called this meeting tonight to review the progress report I e-mailed to you yesterday and to start brainstorming some next steps. As you are both aware, the Ozzzz.com experiment has shown favorable results. Revenues rising by an order of magnitude since we've plugged our neural remapping technology into the site as compared with the six months of running the site in vanilla mode. You've seen the numbers. I think I've proven the point. We know we can capture the minds of babes. I see the next step as being global infiltration across the Web. What do you think? Oh, hey, thanks, Mo." Sam picked up the martini that Mo offered him from the silver Baccarat serving tray.

"Mr. Ben-Hura, your drink…and Mr. Portell, here's yours. Mind if I make myself comfortable?" Mo handed Bob his drink and sat down on the couch so close their thighs touched. Bob fidgeted uncomfortably, drink in hand, first crossing his legs, then uncrossing them, and finally spilling his drink all over his trousers.

Sam quickly stepped out of his chair and turned around, walking toward the far end of his office, in an attempt to stifle his laughter. *Mo, you are the man! Yessss!*

"Oh, my Lord Jesus! Look at what I done. Here, let me clean you up. An important man like you can't be lookin' like that while he's negoshiatin'." Mo snatched the starched white linen napkin that was draped over the silver tray and leaned in close to Bob's face, wiping down the front of his T-shirt. "There now, isn't that better? I am so sorry! I can't tell you how sorry I am. I am so sorry that I will fix you another White Russian that is so strong that it'll feel like it's burnin' a hole in your gut. Just like that cancer that your people injected into my people back in that hospital in Alabama in the 50's. Though I don't suppose you'd remember any of that, being that you were just a kid, now, do you? "

Mo, you're going too far! We haven't even started yet! Sam coughed deliberately and turned around. Mo looked at him as if to say, *"Okay, okay, I got the message."*

"Sorry, Bob. Mo gets a little carried away with his Southern hospitality at times. Sometimes I have to remind him that he doesn't have to shuffle around here in Silicon Valley, like he used to down South. Must be a genetic trait, all of this fussing and shuffling. I'm sure you know what I mean," apologized Sam. Avi looked at Sam. Sam answered him with another look. Avi understood, and remained silent, waiting for a signal.

"Okay, so let's get down to business," continued Sam. "Bob, what we need besides partnership is a sanction to revolutionize the Web. We need to enforce predefined behaviors and thought patterns via the Internet, and you're the head gonzo in that department. So, what do you say, Bob?"

"Yeah, well, I'm not giving the nod until my personal cachet of engineers take a deep look at the code. This can't fail, Sam. I can't fail, and I don't fail. End of story. I say we need more time to look into it before I start broadcasting something with such large-scale implications." Bob said, still looking a bit shell-shocked from his evening cocktail break.

Sam nodded in Avi's direction. *Time to drop more bait.*

"Oh, but Bob," Avi jumped in. "There's something else. You're gonna love it. It's so beautiful! You know all of the little gadgets and toys from Ozzzz.com that the kids are so crazy about? In fact, my nieces and nephews at the kibbutz can't seem to get enough of them! Have you checked the sales revenues on the merchandising side of the business? Well, I would suggest you do that. Sales have gone up 1200%, and it's not only because of the neural remapping stuff embedded in Internet content. Sam's provided my guys over in Israel with the code to embed this into tiny microchips—smaller than a grain of birdseed—programmed with any message we want to communicate to subvert their little minds. So what did we do? We went into production, that's what. We popped them into all of the toys that the Ozzzz.com kids are buying."

"Hmmm. So, what I'm hearing is that the kids get the whammy all the time, not only while they're on the 'Net, but while they're prancing around in their ruby slippers or playing with their Cowardly Lion puppets. Yeah, maybe. Hey, Mo, could you make up that second White Russian you promised? I'm thirsty…and this time, keep your filthy bla…uh, this time, could you use a stir-stick?"

"Oh, sure, 'Massa.' Whatever you say. I'll use a stick all right."

Sam watched Mo make his way to the bar to mix a fresh cocktail for Bob. *Mo, for Godssake, you're shuffling. Let's not take this too far! You're a real uncut crystal, Mo.' You're totally amazing, man, but you've gotta reign it in, soften it up.*

Mo returned with a glass filled with a rich, dark liquid teeming with ice cubes.

"What's this? I asked for a White Russian. Didn't you hear me? This looks like a Black Russian to me," complained Bob, looking irritable.

"Oh, it's just as sweet. Trust me! And you know, you can always pretend it's white inside. Go ahead, Mr. Portell, give it a try, just for the sake of my ancestors."

Bob winced, and put the drink down.

"Look, forget about it, okay? This is really annoying me, Sam. Can't we ask him to leave? Anyway, I want to hear more about these microchips, this nanotechnology. How far will it go, Avi? I mean, are we actually going to be able to seed these in everything, so that no one will even know that they've been touched by it?"

"Bob, we can do anything we want to do. We can alter DNA. Your people know all about that, I understand. We just need distribution!" Avi answered.

"Okay, I get it, but I'm just reluctant to jump in with both feet. Call it skepticism, or attribute it to my conservative streak, but…"

"I know it's not invented here—meaning by you and your multi-national brain trust," Sam said. *It was time to play hardball.* "Give it up, Bob. You've got to give up a little control to get a lot more. Here's your opportunity. Genetic re-engineering. Those are the implications. Ask Mo about that. Hey, Mo what do you know about that subject. Go ahead, tell him what you know."

"Well, Mr. Portell, I honestly don't know much at all from a scientific standpoint. But I can tell you that my father and his uncle died of cancer. And it wasn't because of natural selection, either. No way. Remember those genetic engineering centers your family funded back in the 1950s—Grant and Lucie W. Portell? Right there on the plaques at the Birmingham Center for Family Planning. Remember how those poor black folk and those poor Indian folk were sterilized and then shot up with stuff they were told would make them fight off the flu for the rest of their lives. Remember all that? Did your daddy tell you those bedtime stories? About my papa and my Uncle Clarence over in Alabama? That's what I know, and I am not afraid of talking about it, either."

"Yah, and I won't and can't even bring myself to start on your family's dealings with Germany in the middle of the last century," said Avi, choking back a long-suppressed rage.

"So," said Sam. "We blow the lid, or you belly up to the bar. Pick your poison. A Kamikaze or a Black Russian?"

Bob sat up on the edge of his seat and lunged for the Black Russian he had set on the table beside him. He drank it to the dregs.

"Global neural remapping and gene-altering nanotechnology over the Internet." His chin sank to his chest and he pinched the bridge of his nose with two fingers.

A sweeping upset. Sam tapped the air with his palm, high-fiving Mo and Avi silently. He glanced over at Bob who looked like someone about to enter the maw of a famished, many-headed mutant beast.

"So the Wicked Witch laughed to herself, and thought, 'I can still make her my slave, for she does not know how to use her power.'"

From The Wonderful Wizard of Oz, by Frank Baum, originally published in 1900.

Chapter 23

Damaged Goods

Ever since the humiliating scene with the ruby red slippers, Caitlin made every effort to avoid contact with as many of her coworkers as possible unless absolutely necessary, and even then, she relied on voice-mail and e-mail as much as was practical. The next thing looming on the horizon was the launch party next week, which would probably turn into another embarrassing three-ring marketing circus, no doubt. As the focal point for Ozzzz.com's new spin, the pressure was on for her to dazzle and delight, except that she didn't feel particularly dazzling or delightful these days. Today, she had to meet with Bambi to discuss Virtual Dorothy's role in the launch party. She was hoping that Bambi's schedule would divert her attention, o*r that maybe she'd get food poisoning at lunch.* The other irritant was Sam. He kept walking past her office, sometimes simply nodding in her direction, and at other times, she could swear he was blowing air kisses. Once or twice since their interlude, he set one foot over the threshold of her doorway and gave her a smile and meaningful eye contact. Every time Sam came within 20 feet of her, Caitlin experienced a major meltdown.

I am so drawn to you, Sam, and I can't deal with it. What is it? I've never, ever felt this way. I feel like I should be in some 12-step program! Somewhere she had heard of SLAA…Sex and Love Addicts Anonymous. Maybe it was time to find the Silicon Valley chapter. But was that it, really? It sure didn't feel anything like her relationship with Kent or any of the other guys she dated in high school and college.

Caitlin checked her e-mail. *Oh no, there was one from Bambi!* She hadn't forgotten, and there obviously had been no lurking bacteria in her usual tuna salad lunch.

Mime-Version: 1.0
Date: Wednesday, 25 Apr 2000 14:33:16 -0800
To: cleary@ozzzz.com
From: Bambi Rose<brose@ozzzz.com>
Subject: Meeting/Dinner party
Status:

Hello, Caitlin,
I realize that we scheduled a meeting today at 3:30 to discuss your role in the launch party. If you don't mind, I'd like to change the schedule slightly. I'm having a women's dinner party tonight at my house—very cas—and I would love for you to be there. I thought that we could get together around 6:30 and have our meeting over cocktails for an hour before everyone arrives. I trust that'll work out for you.

Very sincerely,
Bambi

Silicon Valley was not the land of freedom and choice, that was obvious to Caitlin. At half past six, Caitlin pulled up to the Rococo wrought iron gate that protected Bambi Rose's estate. The gates parted automatically, detecting the presence of Caitlin's car, and the ethereal sound of a harp rose up to accompany her around the circular driveway. *The place looks like a movie set!* In the center of the immaculately trimmed circular lawn was a life-sized statue of the Greek goddess, Diana, a gold-tipped arrow drawn taut against her bow. About 50 feet in front of Diana stood a marble stag, its head turned toward the goddess, as if it were pleading for one more chance before having its hindquarters pierced by the inevitable missile.

Caitlin parked her car, walked to the front door, and rang the doorbell. This time, instead of harp music, Pachelbel's Canon in D announced her arrival. The two massive carved doors swung open, and Luz, a tiny Latina, appeared, greeting Caitlin with a broad smile. Luz walked Caitlin to the livingroom.

Caitlin was stunned by the opulence that surrounded her. There were textures of every description, from velvets to silks to gleaming silver and stained glass, all set off by a deep, jewel-like palette of mauve, russet, moss green, and gold.

"Please, have a seat. Mees Bambi will be here shortly. In the meantime, can I offer you a drink…a glass of white wine, some champagne, a martini, perhaps?" said Luz.

Oh, no! I'm not touching another martini as long as I live! "White wine would be lovely, thank you." Caitlin settled herself into a gilt throne-like chair that looked like it had been custom-carved for a Spanish princess.

Luz disappeared to fetch the wine. Caitlin felt like she could spend hours studying the artifacts in this room. It was pure visual gluttony. *So this is what people around here did with their stock option jackpots! How in the world does Bambi even find the time to conceive of all this?* Caitlin's eyes traversed the room, resting on an inscription that circumscribed the room's domed stained glass ceiling. She couldn't quite make out what was written…it was certainly not any language she could recognize, though it did have a vaguely Latinate ring to it, and it seemed as if there were some mathematical symbols imbedded in the message as well.

"I hope I haven't kept you waiting long!" chimed Bambi, handing Caitlin a chilled glass of white wine in a long-stemmed violet crystal glass. "You seem to have a fascination for the inscription around my ceiling."

"Oh, I was trying to figure out what language that might be."

"Actually, it's a very special language. It's not something that everyone is privy to. You might call it an ancient programming language. You know, C++ with a little dash of alchemy."

"Well, it sounds very mysterious. I don't suppose you'd venture to tell me what the inscription means?"

"You'll find out in due time. It's one of my private little games, Caitlin. I like to keep people on edge a bit and drop the clues in a very subtle way. That's something I picked up from your dear friend, Sam."

"My dear…what?" Caitlin quickly sipped some wine.

"Your not-so-secret admirer, your loyal devotee, your follower… mmmm…and maybe your…paramour. Call him what you will!"

"Oh, Sam's nothing of the kind. We've just been working…"

"Yes, I know, dear…very hard and very closely. To change the subject, let's chat for a minute about the launch party. First of all, have you ever been to one?"

"Well, no, I don't believe I have. What, exactly, is the point?"

"Oh, you are technical, aren't you…not a drop of marketing savvy in your sweet young body!"

Caitlin's cheeks flushed. She didn't know whether she was embarrassed or upset by the comment.

"It's all hype. Branding! Remember that term? We are going to make the biggest splash in the industry with the introduction of Virtual Dorothy, the first true Internet personality."

"But, there's nothing really innovative or new about something like that! You can see that on just about any site these days with live streaming videos, talking heads, animations, you name the technology!"

"Oh, but my dear naïve one, it has zilch to do with technology, and everything to do with…oh, here it comes again…Branding! Virtual Dorothy is our creation, our Galatea. She doesn't really exist, of course, but boy, she is some powerful presence. The kids won't be able to live without her. She will be friend, advisor, playmate, teacher, parent, and mentor to them. That's what we're shooting for."

"Okay, well, I'll buy that. So what exactly is it that's expected of me, other than limping around in those toe-crushing ruby slippers?"

"Caitlin, I'm having an identical pair made in your shoe size, so don't let that become an issue. Besides, those shoes are a collector's item! What you need to do is simply be YOU! Your sweet, homespun, innocent, down-to-earth self…with a little polish and sophistication, of course. I know you can do that much! I'll handle the details. Listen, it's going on 7:30. The ladies will be here any minute, so let's call it a day. I need to check on dinner. Luz will be bringing in some finger food, so help yourself. And, in the meantime, just for fun, maybe you can figure out my inscription."

Inside of fifteen minutes, Caitlin found herself seated at a six-foot long table festooned with ten different kinds of orchids, baskets of freshly baked sourdough bread studded with olives and walnuts, and huge serving platters brimming over with colorful salads, braised vegetables, and seafood of every description. She was surrounded by 11 other women, including Bambi, representing various ages and personal styles, all of them highly embellished in some way. Not one of the women could be described as demure or unsophisticated. The assembled party ranged from the slightly overweight and flamboyant 40-something woman who called herself Joannie, to Jaqui, a Cher clone in a tiger-stripe capri pantsuit. Caitlin, who had adopted the white shirt and khakis dotcom look since settling in the valley, felt a tad too austere for this type of gathering, but decided to dig in and enjoy the lobster, something she hadn't had since March. Caitlin nudged the serving platter slightly toward her, and in the process, noticed a small piece of electronic equipment, round and flat like those wafer candies she adored as a child. It looked like a microphone. In fact, she was sure it was. Caitlin picked it up and examined it.

"Caitlin, are you enjoying the lobster? We had it flown in from your home state this morning. Oh, what have you got there?" Bambi leaned over and practically snatched the receiver out of Caitlin's hand.

"It looks like some sort of electronic device…a mike or something," ventured Caitlin.

"Oh that! I have those all over the house. They generate negative ions, so the air stays clean."

"Oh, I see. I don't think I've ever seen them that small. It does look like a microphone, though."

"Caitlin, I know you need more wine. So, here let me fill your glass, and you drink up now!" Bambi filled Caitlin's wineglass to the top, forcing her to take huge gulps to prevent spillage.

"Girls, girls! I'd like to propose a toast to our first-time guest, Caitlin Leary, the belle of Ozzzz.com…Here's the face that's launched a thousand Websites!" Bambi stood up and raised her glass. All of her friends followed suit, clinking glass with their neighbors and winking and whispering while they sent patronizing smiles Caitlin's way.

Caitlin threw out a perfunctory smile and continued to savor the sweet lobster soaked in garlicky butter. At least the evening wasn't a total loss.

"So, Maddy, how are you doing with your new therapist?" Bambi directed her question at a gaunt blonde with huge blue circles under her eyes. Caitlin watched her swaying side to side as she clung to the table to steady herself. *A few too many martoonies for Maddy!*

"Oh, she's great. We're doing something called 'cellular deprogramming.' She taps me on the shoulder every time I go into crisis over Sam. It's supposed to confuse my nervous system and zap any emotional response I have whenever I think of him. I'm not sure if it's kicked in yet, though. I put a knife through a photo I had of him the other night."

Caitlin's eyes widened.

"Oh, I do that all the time...aiming right for his manhood, if you know what I mean," laughed Bambi.

"Speaking of Rambo," piped up a very petite woman with a tiny childlike voice, "What's this I'm hearing through the grapevine about his latest conquest? I hear she's the geeky babe he's been splashing all over the Ozzzz.com site."

"Yeah, Virtual Dorothy, our first Internet starlet! Actually, she is kinda sweet in a sort of unsophisticated way...and obviously clueless about what's in store for her with Sam. Oh well, I guess she'll just have to learn the hard way like we did, poor pathetic creature!" sighed Joannie.

Caitlin slid down into her chair, hoping that no one would notice the resemblance between her and her virtual Web personality. Well, they did plaster on an awful lot of makeup and made her wear her hair in those repulsive pigtails, so maybe no one would catch on. Most of Bambi's guests were pretty tipsy at this point anyway, so she probably wouldn't be found out.

"Caitlin, would you like a little more wine? You seem awfully tense. Here, have a splash of this rich, sensuous cabernet and just let your hair down. You're among friends, dear!" Bambi filled Caitlin's glass to the brim.

Caitlin grabbed the crystal stem and bolted down the wine, ruing the day she accepted the offer to work at Ozzzz.com.

Bambi stood up and tapped her glass with her knife.

"Ladies, ladies…I want to propose a toast to a new member of our circle. Though she's young, she's been fully initiated into the ways of the Valley and, I have no doubt, can be a tremendous asset to our group in our mission to propagate our truth. To Caitlin— may you discover the courageous voice within you that speaks the truth of your heart to the world forever and always!"

"Goddess bless!" chimed the women in unison, raising their glasses in Caitlin's honor.

Caitlin's temples throbbed. She slammed her right fist down, sending a reverberation up and down the length of the table. Glasses wobbled. The silverware jumped. And the rosebuds popped out of their vases.

"All right! I've had enough. I'm tired of the sly looks, the insinuations, and the gossip. Yes, goddam it, I slept with Sam Thorne, just like all the rest of you. And, and, and…" Caitlin lost it, completely. She felt someone on her left put a perfumed arm around her shoulder and hold her, "and I'm so mortified. I feel like, like I'm going mad! I'm losing my mind. That man's done something to me. It's like he's cast a spell on me."

"Oh, hon! It's okay, really. We're all here for you. I can set you up with my therapist. Look, why don't you join up with us. We kind of have this mission…to, ummm, how should I say this kindly… nuke the bum," said Jaqui, rubbing Caitlin's shoulder.

"Absolutely. And Caitlin, with your brains and inside knowledge, you can be an amazing asset. We're counting on you, sister!" added Bambi. "So, let's finish up that toast! To the fall of the evil Mr. Thorne and the resurrection of the wounded sisters of Silicon Valley!"

"'Send me back to Kansas where my Aunt Em and Uncle Henry are,'" she answered earnestly. 'I don't like your country, although it is very beautiful.'"

From The Wonderful Wizard of Oz, by Frank Baum, originally published in 1900.

Chapter 24

Sanctuary

The decisive clicking of the gate into locked mode silenced the trill of angelic harp music as Caitlin steered her car past the detector out into the dark country roads of Woodside. She drove half a mile and, unable to endure the tormenting throbbing around her temples, pulled over onto the shoulder, so that her car was shielded by the shadows cast by a thicket of honeysuckle bushes. Caitlin fumbled for her purse, whose contents had spilled onto the floorboard of the passenger side of her car. Among the jumble of notes, daytimer, hairbrush, and make-up, she managed to fish out her cell phone and, in the comforting darkness, punched in the number from memory, hoping she'd gotten it right. Leaning back into the headrest, she clutched the phone close to her ear, praying there would be an answer.

"Caitlin!" the voice said with certainty while the first ring still hung in the air.

"How did you know?"

"Caitlin…you were on my radar screen. I told you that it works that way with me. Are you all right? Are you safe? Where are you?"

"Trini…No to your first question, yes to your second, and in Woodside near Buffalo's, right on 84 to answer your third. I think I've had way, way too much to drink tonight and way, way too much to digest. My head feels like it's ready to detonate."

"Listen, don't move. Put on the radio, sleep, whatever, but don't budge that car another inch. I'm coming over right this minute."

"Trini, Trini, why are you…"

"Don't ask me questions you already know the answer to, . I'll be there in fifteen minutes, *seguro*!"

The scent of the intoxicating honeysuckle bushes lulled Caitlin to a gentle sleep, temporarily lifting her out of her reality into a place of simplicity and sweet repose.

It seemed as though she traveled for a very long time in that other realm until she was awakened by the sound of gravel crunching under Trini's shoes as he walked toward her car, a backpack slung over one shoulder. He slid into the seat next to her, and leaning over, cupped his hand under the base of her head and kissed her on the forehead. Caitlin felt blurry, but comforted by his presence.

"*Niña*, here, have some of this…some herbal tea *para las chicas emborrachadas*…chamomile, valerian, orange blossom, and mint. And if that doesn't do the trick, I brought some Ibuprofen too." Trini pulled a sleek silver thermos out of his backpack and poured

Caitlin a cup of tea. She held the thermos mug with both hands, taking in the steam for a moment and then sipping the hot, therapeutic beverage.

"Ooooh, Trini, I'm in a bad way! I can't believe what's been happening to my life since I've come to Silicon Valley. Life used to be fairly simple...studying, visiting my friends and parents at home, going to movies and gallery openings with Kent. Hey, Trini, do I look wasted and used up? Now, tell me the truth!"

"*Preciosa*...I call you that because you are...how can you even ask me a question like that? I look at you and I see nothing but freshness and sincerity. Why are you thinking that way about your-self? Did Sam try to pull something over on you again?"

"Oh, no, Trini. It wasn't that at all. I was at Bambi Rose's home tonight—you may know her—one of the investors at Ozzzz.com. So there I was with half a dozen women who've had their bodies and souls pummeled by Sam Thorne and who are out to get him for it. Big time! And me, terminally honest me! I opened my big mouth and blurted out the whole thing about Sam and me. How could I be so stupid! So now, they think they've recruited me into the sisterhood, into their cause."

"Their cause?"

"Yeah, they're going to have an uprising to knock Thorne off his throne. I have no clue what they plan on doing, but somehow they're thinking that I should be—and want to be—a part of their schemes. Trini, I just came here to learn, to make a few bucks, and experience Silicon Valley. What have I gotten myself into?

The even bigger question is, why me? Oh, God, I sound like I'm whining. Trini, just slap me. Tell me to stop, will you?"

Trini chuckled and curled his arm around her shoulder.

"Caitlin, you can talk all you want around me. Tell me everything or tell me nothing, if you choose. I want you to come with me tonight. Stay at my place. I have an extra futon, and on my word of honor, you will be respected and cared for as you deserve to be."

Too weary to contest Trini's offer or even to analyze his motives, Caitlin flicked away a wandering doubt and followed him to his truck. She noticed as he walked ahead that he had on his mural painting pants…decorated with random splashes and streaks of bright acrylic paint, they looked even more beautiful than the first time she smiled at them…or maybe it was just the wine.

"Net Privacy Law Doesn't Replace Parents" by Lawrence Magid

"The Children's Online Privacy Protection Act mandates that commercial Web sites aimed at children younger than 13 obtain verifiable parental consent 'before collecting, using or disclosing personal information from a child.'

One of the most controversial aspects of the law is how a site obtains parental consent...

...the parent can submit a credit card for verification on the theory that only adults have access to credit card numbers. Disney Online, according to a spokesperson, plans to require parents to verify their identity with a credit card because its site allows kids to post messages on a public bulletin board, which is a form of public disclosure...

The law was enacted after a 1998 FTC report that found that 85 percent of the sites studied collected personal information from consumers, but only 14 percent offered any notice about how the information is used and only 2 percent included a comprehensive privacy policy.

Of the sites in the study aimed at children, 89 percent collected personal information directly from children, but only 54 percent disclosed their information practices and fewer than 10 percent provided for some form of parental control over the collection of information...

...Even with this law in place, it would be reckless for parents to think that all is well just because the government is protecting their children's privacy."

San Francisco Sunday Examiner and Chronicle, Sunday, April 30, 2000

Chapter 25

Overwrought Mothers Enraged about the 'Net (OMEN)

"Jaqueeee! I'm desperate! Can you come over right away? I swear I'm raising a houseful full of cyber-droids. Listen to my voice! I'm so hoarse I can barely talk! I am soooo unglued! I've been yelling at the top of my lungs all night trying to get my girls unhooked from the Internet so they could eat dinner and do their homework. I finally coerced them to go to bed. Jaqui, I need to talk to someone!"

"Sit tight, girlfriend! Don't do anything desperate. I'll be there in a flash."

Charlotte Meyerstone clutched her cell-phone to her breast as if it were her lifeline. *This has got to end! I swear, I am ready to, to, to ...My God, I don't know who my children are anymore!* She collapsed into despairing sobs, beating her fists on her kitchen table. *Someone, please HELP me get my girls back!*

The chiming doorbell propelled Charlotte from her chair. *Jaqui, Thank God!*

"My goodness, Char! I've never seen you like this! You are in a bad way! Oh, look at the mascara running down your cheek!" Jaqui produced a tissue and dabbed her friend's cheeks.

Charlotte forced a smile of gratitude and fell into Jaqui's arms, feeling herself losing it completely. Jaqui was the only person in her life with whom she felt safe acting this way. In spite of her vanities and posings, Jaqui had, over the decade they shared in Silicon Valley, proved to be a compassionate friend, someone Charlotte could rely on for advice, information, and above all, effective action.

"C'mon, let me fix you something to drink, and then you can tell me all about it!" Jaqui led Charlotte to the livingroom, and sat her down on the peach silk chaise lounge, handing her a wad of tissue and arranging some throw pillows around her to make her comfortable. In her usual take-charge way, Jaqui pulled two shot glasses and a decanter of tequila from the liquor cabinet. She poured the drinks and carried them over to Charlotte, who allowed herself to surrender fully to her friend's nurturing and attention.

"Here, slug this down, and lay it on me," said Jaqui, sitting down at Charlotte's feet.

"Jaqui, I am so defeated by this! I'm going insane, I swear it. My kids are completely ignoring me, ignoring their schoolwork, ignoring their Dad…and that's pretty easy…since he's hardly ever home. They won't eat, it's a battle to get them to bed every night, and I just can't deal anymore. All they talk about is Ozzzz.com this and Ozzzz.com that. It's like they're under some sort of spell. And every week, we get these packages from the place…toys, dolls, books.

Their rooms look like a dotcom toy warehouse! I haven't even checked the VISA bill yet. I can't bring myself to open the envelope."

"Have you talked to Tom about this?" asked Jaqui.

"Tom? Tom who? You know what life with Tom Meyerstone is like! You were married to him two wives ago! If he's not out golfing with the guys, he's at some ridiculous launch party. Making frriggin' deals is all he cares about. I swear he forgets he's got a wife and kids when he's away. No, I haven't talked to Tom!"

"Okay, forget Tom. I sure did! So, let's get back to the kids. It sounds like you feel like the kids have kind of wigged out over the 'Net...living in an alternate reality, almost," suggested Jaqui.

"Yeah, that's it exactly. I feel like I don't know who they are anymore. I see Amanda and little Kirsten mesmerized by this Ozzzz.com thing. You should hear them prattling on about how Virtual Dorothy would never eat vegetables, or how Virtual Dorothy owns forty different pairs of ruby slippers, or how Virtual Dorothy plays games on the Internet all day! They're even starting to dress like her, pigtails and all! Jaqui, am I the only mother in this Virtual World who is raising zombie kids? I feel so helpless and alone in this. I give up, I tell you. I give up."

Jaqui got up and started pacing back and forth across Charlotte's handsome new Berber rug. Charlotte felt a rush of encouragement. This is just how Jaqui operated. Feed her the facts, and she would not only help you achieve a profound clarification of the issue, but would also come up with nothing less than a brilliant strategy for resolution. *Bless you, my soul sister!*

"Charlotte, I have something to confide in you, and please, please, promise me that what I have to say goes no further than this room."

"Jaqui, you know you can count on me. After all we've been through together!"

"Okay, then, here it is. Ozzzz.com. You're probably aware of this, I'm sure. The brains and money behind Ozzzz.com is Sam Thorne, king of database software, CEO of Prophet, Inc. Okay, maybe that means nothing to you. It does to me. A great deal. When I was married to your Tom, I reported directly to Sam, back at Prophet. I was his admin…and actually, a little more than that, as it turned out, if you know what I mean! And please, don't hold it against me, Charlotte. I was young and, well, bored with my marriage—no offense to your husband. At any rate, Sam gave me a little gift. No, not a bambino, but something a whole lot worse…a roaring case of gonorrhea. It was more than embarrassing. I had a hell of a lot of explaining to do to Tom Who! I was so enraged by this that I sued Sam for sexual harassment and threatened to leak his vile behavior to the press. To shut me up, he gave me a pittance of a settlement, a few hundred thousand, and threatened to blackball me from the industry. Well, my darling Charlotte, even though I worked hard to marry rich in my new incarnation, I've never quite processed my anger and upset over the Sam Thorne affair, so consider me your able ally. Love may be sweet, but revenge is sweeter yet!"

Charlotte forgot her sorrow for a moment as she tried to digest Jaqui's new disclosure. Adultery or even adulterous thoughts were completely alien to her. Whomever she was attached to at any given time had her total attention, regardless of whether the relationship was flourishing or foundering. She found herself admiring Jaqui even more, both for having the nerve to have an affair behind Tom's back and for standing up to the humiliation she suffered from Sam Thorne.

"Oh, Jaqui, thanks so much for sharing. I will keep my lips sealed, I promise. No one will ever know about this, especially not Tom."

"Oh, don't worry about him. He knows it all, anyway. Let's forget about all that for the moment and draw up a game plan. I know one very special geek who is so clever with the Internet, it's scary. And if he doesn't do his mother's bidding, well, no BMW motorcycle for his birthday in two months. So that said, I'll line up Nathan. Meet me at my house tomorrow around noon, and we'll pow-wow over pizza and Jolt. Oh, and by the way, how does 'Overwrought Mothers Enraged about the 'Net' sound to you?"

"OMEN? I don't get it. I don't get you, Jaqui, but I love you. How come you're not CEO of your own company? I'd be the first one to bet my money on that one!"

". . .and if you wrong us, shall we not revenge?"
William Shakespeare, The Merchant of Venice

Chapter 26

The Hactivists

"NAYYYTHAN!" shouted Jaqui as she ushered Charlotte into the foyer of her newly built home.

"NATHANIEL EVERITT SOMMERS! I COMMAND YOU! Sheez, Charlotte, what does a mother have to do to get her children to pay attention! You know that one well! Okay, one more try."

Jaqui picked her slim cell phone, dialed, and whispered sweetly, "Is this The Ripper? It's your mother. We have some serious negotiation to do over lunch in the kitchen. SO GET YOUR ASS IN GEAR AND GET DOWN HERE NOW!"

"The Ripper? As in Jack the Ripper?" said Charlotte incredulously. "Is that Nathan's nickname? When I was a kid, we had nicknames like Pookie and KissyFace."

"Oh, that's his handle. You know, just like the ham radio operators, except it's a name he uses on the 'Net to stay anonymous in those chatrooms and bulletin boards. I suppose he feels that name pumps up his testosterone. Kids are weird today. In my day, all boys thought about was girls and football."

Nathan bounded loudly down the steps. Jaqui smiled. She hadn't seen her son in a few days. He was looking good, nicely muscled, good skin tone, no acne. She made sure that he would not slide into the stereotypical out-of-body geek look, even if he did have the mind for it, by setting him up with a trainer 4 days a week who led him on grueling mountain bike rides and runs in the Woodside hills followed by an hour of weight-training. She did hate his clothes, though. He was wearing a pair of those hideous baggy shorts that flopped over his knees and looked like they were about to crumple around his ankles any minute, a T-shirt with Latin words circling a sinister looking dragon, and bare feet, festooned with silver rings on every one of his toes.

"Hey, Ripper, you remember Charlotte. C'mon, kid, I've got your favorite pizza down in the kitchen. We have some serious talking to do."

"Hi, Charlotte. Aw, Mom, I was just racking frags—er—scoring points in Quake! Can't I eat later?"

"Rip, this is not about eating. This is about business. Visualize yourself on a cherry red Beemer vrooming through La Honda, putting all of those old bikers out there to shame. And then again, visualize yourself here, no Beemer, on your mountain bike with your trainer barking at you from behind EVERY DAY OF THE WEEK."

"All right, all right. I give up. I'd sure like to know what this is about, though."

"Believe me, son, it's right up your Internet pipeline."

"Mom, how do you know these things?"

"Hey, do I look stupid. Didn't I manage to land you in these incredible digs? It wasn't all looks, you know."

Jaqui led her son by the arm to the kitchen, and Charlotte followed. The table was already set with cheery handpainted stoneware and the kitchen was filled with the smell of garlicky pizza.

Serving up generous hunks of pizza and iced tea, Jaqui got down to business. There was no time to waste. Charlotte needed her. Jaqui realized that since settling into the community here in Woodside, she had a tendency to make Charlotte her project... probably because after so many years of trying to stay ahead of her own personal setbacks, she felt her life had now reached a place of stability and there were no major fixes to make. And, she could empathize with someone who now lived with her ex-husband. Well, okay, so she was a little bored too. Still, Charlotte needed her. Helpless, hapless Charlotte, who tried so hard to be good all the time. Jaqui was pleased to see that at least Charlotte was progressing...she had lost 15 pounds since they started going to kickboxing together and she agreed to start seeing Jaqui's therapist to help her get over her doormat complex. This issue with the children was a huge one for Charlotte. This was something Jaqui could relate to, being a mother herself. And she was ready to coach her all the way, stand by her, hold her hand, even step in and do it for her, if she ran out of juice (and Jaqui felt she would).

"Jaqui, I don't understand what your son has to do with all this. He's just a kid!" said Charlotte.

"Char, Rip, I have brought you together because on this side of the table, we have a huge worldwide problem—Char—and on the other side of the table—we have the brilliant mind—Rip—who will offer a hell of a solution. So, Rip, listen up, and tell me if we can do this. Char's little girls, you know them, Amanda and Kirsten have been walking around the house like e-zombies. You know, kind of like you used to be. Naturally, Charlotte, who is a concerned mother, just like I was and am concerned about you, my love, needs your help,"

"Yeah, okay. I get it, but why doesn't she send those girls to ballet class or something?" offered Nathan.

"No, no, no. It's way, way, way beyond that. These kids are like, brainwashed. Brainwashed. Braindead. Gonzo. No see 'um. And you know why? It's that Ozzzz.com site. Their brain cells know only the language of Ozzzz.com. Buy this. Order that. Play these games till your fingers bleed and rack up Mom and Dad's credit card, by the millisecond."

"Heh, heh. That's pretty clever. Great way to get rich off of dumb little kids, and their even dumber parents!"

"I beg your pardon. My children are not..." Charlotte started to protest.

"Char, SHUT UP. He's right. See how his mind works. You give him the broad sweep. He gets it. Sorry, Rip. Here, have another slice. Ice tea, my Einstein?"

"Einstein didn't do anything important. He didn't even use a computer."

"Okay, then, my Mark Andreissen Junior!"

"That's more like it, Mom!"

"Anyway, back to matters at hand. Remember back in February, when that mysterious hacker brought Yahoo, Amazon, and eBay to their knees? What did they call it? Oh, yeah, 'distributed denial of service.' I like the sound of that. I wonder how they did that?"

"Mom, that was a cinch. All we, I mean they, had to do was hack into a couple of servers and blast the sites with millions of messages,"

"Rip, did I hear you say 'we'?"

"Uh, no. I dunno. Maybe you're hearing things. Yeah, anyway, that's cake!"

"Okay, hear no evil. I love you," Jaqui grabbed her son's chin and wagged it till his face turned scarlet. "Can you figure out how to do this? Can you do this from some other place, in other words, not in this house, not on the computer Ray bought you? If he found out it was you, we'd be sleeping under the freeway with our shopping cart—a real one—in no time."

"The answer is yes and yes. I think you forgot to ask me one more question. Will I do this—that is, pull the plug from Ozzzz.com."

"Well?"

"If I have time. Hey, mom, whatcha got for dessert?"

"I thought you loved doing this kind of thing! Listen. Here's how it works. We cut down personal training to three days a week. You'll have more time. And don't forget about the birthday wheels! No hacking, no wheels. Understood?"

"Eh, yeah. I get it. Charlotte, I'll get your girls off the Net and back in front of the TV with their Barbies in no time. I promise. I do. Hey, Mom, it's been a pleasure doing business with you. Could I have some of that Vermont ice cream?"

"All you want, sweetest."

Nathan grabbed a half-gallon of chocolate ice cream from the freezer and a soupspoon and ran off to his room.

"Jaqui, what in the world is going on? All I wanted was some support, some direction. I certainly didn't expect you to devise this crazy scheme to crash the Internet!" cried out Charlotte, once she was
certain that Nathan was beyond earshot.

"Char, relax. Leave it all to me. First of all, we're not out to crash the Internet. I just want to cause Sam Thorne a little bit of public discomfort. It's such an opportunity! And, secondly, I want to help you out. I want you to have your kids back. Besides, you're not alone, believe me! Do you think other moms out there aren't just as concerned, maybe even outraged by the effect sites like Ozzzz.com are having on their families? Next time you take Amanda to Middle

School, count the number of pairs of red glitter high-heeled sneakers you see running across the playground…or the wash-off Ozzzz.com tattoos, or the Ozzzz.com lunchboxes. It's insidious!"

"You know, you're right. I'm not the only one, and if there ever were a cause worth fighting for in my life, this one is! I'm with you. But, for God's sake, Jaqui, please be careful. Please make sure Nathan is safe."

"Don't worry about a thing. Let's stay close. Keep your cell with you at all times. Okay, so Ozzzz.com, get ready for the OMEN!"

"Amen, the OMEN!"

"Little strokes
Fell great oaks."
Benjamin Franklin

Chapter 27

Denial

May 5, 2000

Palo Alto, CA—Ozzzz.com, the popular children's Website, was brought down by an unidentified hacker for a record 12 hours yesterday. This is the longest sustained hacker attack in the history of the Internet. There were no other incidents reported with similar high-traffic sites.

A technical spokesperson from Ozzzz.com stated that this was a classic case of distributed denial of service. Similar cyber sabotage schemes temporarily disabled major e-commerce sites earlier this year, affecting Yahoo!, Amazon.com, eBay, ZDNet, and others. Recently, a 16-year-old Montreal boy, who called himself "Mafia Boy," was identified as the hacker responsible for halting the CNN site this February. Distributed denial of service is generally executed by a group of hackers who could be scattered all over the globe. Their strategy is to drown the servers with such a huge volume of "crank calls," or "hits," that the servers don't have the processing time or bandwidth to handle legitimate calls.

"We at Ozzzz.com are doing everything in our power to ensure that our global community of children get the kind of service they have a right to enjoy. We can't imagine that anyone with a conscience would attack a harmless children's Website and deprive millions of young people of a forum for learning valuable skills that will help them become responsible cyber-citizens of the future," said Ozzzz.com CEO Sam Thorne. Among the top ten most successful techno-tycoons in the world, Thorne is best known for his highly successful company, The Prophet Corporation, provider of powerful relational database software deployed by 90 percent of business and government institutions worldwide.

Thorne did not disclose estimated losses resulting from the site shutdown. He did indicate that the technical staff at Ozzzz.com was attempting to track down the perpetrators, but so far have made no significant progress.

According to the National Internet Protection Council, anyone who knowingly transmits codes, commands, or programs without authorization to a secure computer and intentionally causes damage can be prosecuted. The penalty for such crimes ranges from a minimum of six months imprisonment to a maximum of five years. Fines start at $250,000 to double the amount of losses incurred by the victimized organization.

"A number of psychologists and sociologists are beginning to worry that the generation that is growing up in simulated worlds and becoming comfortable with the idea of buying access to cultural commodities and lived experiences might not have sufficient emotional experience to empathize."

Jeremy Rifkin, The Age of Access

Chapter 28

Backlash

534 e-mails, and at least 60% of them marked urgent! Caitlin scanned the sender and subject list quickly…too many unkind phrases from unknown senders!

Mime-Version: 1.0
Date: Tues, 2 May 2 2000 6:58:16 -0800
To: webmistress@ozzzz.com
From: Anne Wornecki (annew@aol.com)
Subject: Reprehensible!
Status:

To whom it may concern,
This is reprehensible! As an elementary school teacher in Glen Falls, Idaho, who is attempting to steer children toward a humane, community-oriented view of life, I am mortified that a site like Ozzzz.com is allowed to flourish on the Internet. My students have been so thoroughly brainwashed by Corporate America that they have lost all sense of reality. All of their innocence and curiosity has been replaced by rampant consumerism and brand-worship.

I might add that this syndrome has appeared to have worsened since the introduction of that vile creation, Virtual Dorothy.

Mime-Version: 1.0
Date: Tues, 2 May 2 2000 10:13:16 -0800
To: webmistress@ozzzz.com
From: Cathy Morgenthal <cmorgenthal@plannet.com>
Subject: Delete Dorothy
Status:

To the corporate elite at Ozzzz.com,

Since the introduction of Virtual Dorothy to the Ozzzz.com Website, my monthly bill for your site has quadrupled. The message seems to be—play more "pay-by-the minute" games, buy more useless logo-wear, and drive your parents to the welfare office. Cancel

my account this instant! Whoever this Dorothy is—real, or digital—I say hit the delete key right now!

Mime-Version: 1.0
Date: Tues, 2 May 2 2000 12:47:16 -0800
To: webmistress@ozzzz.com
From: Bill Sanremo <bsanremo@cs.net>
Subject: Blacklist Ozzzz.com
Status:

Hey, you greedy, insidious bastards!

Cancel my kid's subscription to your site. NOW. And if it doesn't happen in the next five minutes—well, I'll leave that to your imagination. Your site sucks. My kid doesn't even speak to me anymore because he's so wrapped up in this Ozzzz.com thing. That's all he talks about. I'm pulling the plug. NOW. And you can tell that airhead Dorothy that she's polluting cyberspace!

Mime-Version: 1.0
Date: Tues, 2 May 2 2000 16:06:16 -0800
To: webmistress@ozzzz.com
From: Omen <omen@biglink.com>
Subject: This is war!
Status:

OMEN—Overwrought Mothers Against the Net—hereby
declares war on Ozzzz.com. Our organization of concerned mothers is sounding the battle cry to put an end to the exploitative tactics
of Ozzzz.com. You are infecting the minds of our children with
dangerous consumerist obsessions and preventing them from
living balanced and healthy lives. Mothers worldwide, unite!
Let's stop the beast from devouring our children!

The end of her life as she knew it! Caitlin ran to the ladies' room and furiously set to scrubbing her face and hands as if she had emerged from a long swim in the underground sewers of Silicon Valley. She looked up at her wet face, red and raw from the hot water and desperate tears. At that moment, the door swung open, and in walked Bambi.

"What the hell happened to you?" Bambi stood before the dripping Caitlin and shoved a handful of paper towels into her hand. "Okay, okay, you don't have to say word one. It was Sam again. Old Sam the Ram up to his old tricks. Girl, when are you going to learn?"

"Bambi, no. No, it's not Sam. It's me! My life's over, I'm telling you. I am a complete disaster. The whole world despises me!"

"God, you're hard on yourself! Hey, I think you're all right. Boy, that man sure knows how to damage a little girl's confidence, doesn't he!"

"Bambi. It's more serious than that. I'm telling you, we—Ozzzz.com—is in deep trouble. They hate me. All those parents and teachers think I'm some digitally created monster that's twisting their children's minds. I got over 500 hate e-mails today. It's like a worldwide lynch mob!"

"What! Hate e-mails? I don't get it. What's going on? Forward them to me immediately! And put on some make-up for God's sake. You're supposed to look fresh and perky. So, come on, already, you know how to do perky!"

"Bambi, stop. Stop right now. I am not an actress. I am not a cartoon character! I am not your fantasy creation, your Liza

Doolittle! I'm technical director here, godddam it! Just let me do my real job!" Caitlin ripped through her hair with a brush and flashed a smoldering look at Bambi. "I'm finished. No more Virtual Dorothy for me. I want nothing more to do with it, and I'll send you those e-mails. I hope you find them pleasant bedtime reading!"

"Problems are the price of progress."

Charles Kettering, Strategy and Business, 1997.

Chapter 29

Blackout

Raj stood trembling at the threshold of Caitlin's office, gripping the doorjamb with white knuckles.

"Caitlin! They've brought us to our knees! We're dead in the water. Sam will go ballistic!" Raj squealed.

Caitlin jumped to her feet. She had just come back from another meeting about leveraged branding and merchandising Virtual Dorothy and hadn't had a moment to even check her e-mail.

"Raj, you look like your dog just up and keeled over. Get a grip! What's going on?"

"Caitlin, it's the gray hats. They got to our site. Ozzzz.com's been down for two hours. They're jamming the pipes, and, sweet lady, it's your ass that's on the line!"

"Wha, whaaaat! Oh, for God's sake, here I've been wasting my time listening to this ridiculous marketing hype for two hours instead of doing my real job. Raj, we're calling an emergency staff meeting. Get on my phone and page the IT department into the WOC right NOW! I'll meet you over there in five minutes, do you hear me?"

As Caitlin flew down the long corridor to the Web Operation Center, she heard swift footsteps thundering on the marble floors behind her.

"Caitlin! Goddam you, I command you to stop! NOW!"

Caitlin lurched to a halt, filled with dread. She felt a powerful grip bearing down so hard on her left shoulder that she couldn't have taken another step if she tried.

"Turn around and look at me!"

Caitlin turned. Sam Thorne's angry eyes drilled into her skull. Caitlin was paralyzed and appalled. This was a face of Sam she had never witnessed before, and it both outraged and repulsed her.

"Look, you little MIT smartass, I am holding you personally account-able for any loss of profit endured by MY company during this episode. I don't know how you thought you would escape that responsibility! Get your geek squad in gear, and get that site back up. If it's not up in twenty minutes, I'll personally see to it that you're laughed out of Silicon Valley. I mean, really, who in their right mind would hire that bimbo, Virtual Dorothy, for a serious technical position?"

Caitlin felt tears of rage threatening to boil over and fought them with every fiber of strength she could muster. *He could actually do this—ruin someone for life. And he has. He's actually done this kind of thing to people. Those women were telling the truth!*

Without a word, Caitlin turned on her heels and made a beeline to the WOC, with Sam only inches away. She could feel him deliriously spewing his rage-fouled breath behind her neck.

Caitlin buzzed the security door to the WOC and walked in. The data center was abuzz with network gnomes and info-systems trolls, all gathered around the racks of network servers that lined the back wall of the cavernous room. This was the class of geeks who led profoundly asocial mole-like existences, locked in a 55-degree room with linoleum floors, metal racks stacked high with processors and monitors humming their monotonous white noise cantata 24 by 7! *God, thought Caitlin, these poor souls who are always taken for granted, always blamed when things go wrong, are about to be reamed by Sam.* She tried to force a compassionate, sympathetic smile in an effort to rouse their spirits, as she rallied them together.

"Okay, guys, this is a five-alarm fire! What's up? From what Raj said, it looks like a distributed denial of services. They've been pounding us with crank calls for over two hours! Justin and Paul, check to see if they're jamming all of the servers. Seymour, keep on monitoring to see if you can trace the calls and make sure all of the activity is logged."

"Caitlin," boomed Sam. All of the hardware in the WOC rattled. "Don't think you're even this close to saving your skin. Where the hell were you two hours ago, you lame, self-serving prima donna! When you're done in here, I want to see you in my office."

Caitlin felt herself shriveling up in front of her direct reports. The most the boys could offer in the way of support was to turn their eyes away, pretending to be absorbed in the nearest monitor or staring at the red squiggles in the shiny black linoleum. Caitlin collapsed in a chair that someone had silently offered her and buried her head in her hands. She felt someone hesitantly tapping on her shoulder. Raising her head, she saw that a chubby hand extended a cold can of Jolt to her. She took a few swigs, feeling the carbonation sting her nose and the caffeine swirling in her bloodstream.

Seymour, the IT Director and most senior member of the group at the age of 27, was crouching down next to Caitlin.

"Eh, Caitlin, I don't want to throw the guys off track, but I think we're all dead meat here. I've been all over this since it hit the site. Whoever it is that's causing the jam has an army of privates taking orders from colonels scattered all over the world. I just don't get it! It's not like we're E-trade, just a bloody kid's site. If I were you, I'd walk. Hey, I've got a couple of great leads on some start-ups if you're interested."

"Seymour, thanks for the information, but what do I tell Sam? Your answer isn't good enough!" said Caitlin, beginning to under-stand why people who stared at monitors 12 hours a day drank Jolt.

"Wait a minute. I have an idea—it's kind of lame, but it'll at least get Sam off your—I mean our backs for a while. I'll just grab the mirror site and load to my personal server, which is hooked up to a local ISP with a slightly different URL. Sam won't even notice. He sort of loses it when he's this mad. I've been around him long enough to know—usually it's either the martinis or a couple of lines of snow."

"But what about the e-commerce functions? You won't be able to do all that in 20 minutes!"

"I just put the basic site up now and we'll deal with the commerce side later. Give me a moment. I'll get Kenny and Sampo set up, and I'll come with you to Sam's office. We'll snow him. Trust me. I've been around long enough to know that a little condescension goes a long way. I'll talk way over his head. Sam's an intelligent guy, but he's no bit-twiddler."

"Seymour, you're a prince. I guess it's us against them, isn't it? I guess that's what pushes the pulse of the Valley, doesn't it?"

"Spy on Anyone! See everything that happens on any-body's computer—from the websites they visit to 'private' AOL chats!"

Internet ad for iSpyNow, remote spy software, July, 2002.

Chapter 30

Getting it Up, Keeping it Up!

"You're ten minutes late, Caitlin! And I asked you to come alone, Goddamit!" Sam lurched out of his chair, slamming a silver paperweight in the shape of a ram with curled horns on top of his custom-built 28-inch monitor.

"Excuse me, Sam, but it is precisely 20 minutes to the second from the time you issued your request for Caitlin to appear at your office, and, if I may be so bold, you only asked her to appear at your office, never indicating your desire that she come unescorted," Seymour said, raising one finger and one eyebrow for emphasis.

Sam sat down abruptly, swiveling his chair from side to side and glared first at Seymour and then at Caitlin.

"Seymour, get your fat ass back in that WOC."

"Again, excuse me sir, but you might just be interested in some information that Caitlin and I have to share with you. It's about the site." Seymour stopped. *Ah, he's baiting him*, Caitlin thought. She was so relieved that Seymour had accompanied her! Without him,

Caitlin imagined herself stammering, stuttering and morphing into the slobbering bimbo she was accused of being.

"Yeah, all right. What is it? Did you get it up? Did you? Have you ever gotten it up in your life, Seymour?"

"Sam, I don't have any inkling of what you mean. If you would simply allow me to take that little mouse of yours and point it at this browser, you will get the thrill of your life. See, we managed to get it up now, didn't we? It didn't take long at all."

The Ozzzz.com site popped onto Sam's monitor. Caitlin felt the knots loosen in the back of her neck. Sam sank back into his chair, trying to look unimpressed.

"That's your goddam job—to keep it up. I don't want to see this happen again! Seymour, get out of my sight. I need to talk to your former super—"

Caitlin Leary, please call the WOC at extension 911. Caitlin Leary, please call the WOC at extension 911. The receptionist's crisp voice stopped Sam, mid-sentence. He poked a button on his conference phone.

"She's in a meeting!"

"Caitlin! Caitlin there? It's Sampo. I think I've tracked 'em down!"

"You mean the hackers? Well, what gives?" Sam commanded.

Caitlin and Seymour clustered around the triangular conference phone.

"Well, I don't know exactly how to put this to you, Sam, but we over at the WOC have traced it to three internal systems," said Sampo.

"What! So, am I to assume that this is an inside job? Whose systems?" demanded Sam.

"Oh, uh, here's the list we've come up with so far—Rajit Kalipat, Guy Tinker, and J.W. Nielsen."

"Sampo, are you sure? 100% sure?"

"I won't say that all the messages were issued by those machines, but we've determined that about 50% of them were."

"Listen, keep after it. I need more information. Somehow, this doesn't sit right with me. Continue the trace and call me directly— not Caitlin—if you come up with any additional info."

"Okey-doke, Sam. We're all over it."

Sam pushed the "Release" button on the triangular conference phone, and remained quiet for a few moments. Caitlin couldn't read him. She had no idea where she stood, whether she should stand there and await further orders and possibly endure more horsewhipping humiliation, turn around and shut the huge guilded doors of Ozzzz.com behind her forever, or just pick up the raveled threads of her responsibilities and carry on.

"An inside job. I don't believe it. It's a diversionary tactic. Very, very clever indeed. I wonder why they chose those particular individuals' machines? Okay, let's get to the bottom of this. Seymour, back to your post at the WOC. Caitlin, I need a moment with you."

As Seymour shut the door to Sam's office, Caitlin walked over to the lime green Italian sofa and sunk into its contours.

"Caitlin, look, I'm sorry I exploded at you like that. Never mind that I just lost about a million in revenues. I guess it's part of the 'Net game. Hey, how about a martini? You seemed to enjoy those. You haven't forgotten all about that sweet moment, have you?"

Caitlin declined the drink. *No way. I'm sitting here stone sober, and he's not getting within ten feet of me.*

"Caitlin, are you all right? I haven't heard a word from you since you walked in here. Aw, come on, this is just business. Nothing personal. Really. You're safe with me. I promise. Your job is safe, and you are safe. I didn't mean a thing I said to you today. *Amigos?*"

Sam sat down next to Caitlin and extended his hand in a gesture of reconciliation. Caitlin felt herself curl into a tight little ball. Trini's native language coming out of Sam's mouth stung her with its lack of authenticity.

"Sam. If everything's business as usual, then it's business as usual. I have my work cut out for me. If you need me, I'll be at the WOC with the guys. Is there anything else?"

"Caitlin, there's always something else."

Apparently so. That was Sam Thorne, always harboring an agenda, a plan, a scheme. Those women from Woodside were not liars. They were not vindictive harpies. They were victims. I am not one of them!

"In addition to concerns about our kids' safety in the real world, we worry about their trips into cyberspace. When they're on the Internet, they're out in public. Unless we happen to be in the room with them, though, they're out on their own.

Even during their trips to the mall, they're in a well-lighted environment, with friends and within shouting distance of security guards and shopkeepers. In cyberspace, they could be almost anywhere, interacting with just about anyone.

Indeed, there are some dark alleys in cyberspace that are totally inappropriate for children and teens."

"On Computers" by Lawrence Magid, excerpted from the San Francisco Examiner, Sunday, April 2, 2000.

Chapter 31

The Chatroom

"Charlotte, they've just made your introduction. You go, girl! And, oh, don't trip over the wires! " Jaqui Childers propelled her friend through the dusty black curtains, stage left, into the livingrooms of millions of devotees of Eden Winters' Chatroom, the most highly-rated TV talk show to usher in the new millennium.

I'm so proud of you, Charlotte. I've never seen you look more stunning, nor more confident! Jackie watched Charlotte stride across stage in front of the live audience—tight and thin and focused like she's never been before. Charlotte took her place next to Eden Winters, who sat with his palms pressed together under the tip of his nose, as he was about to speak. Jaqui noticed that Eden was attired in a black collarless shirt, tailored black slacks and fine Italian leather ankle boots—sober, tasteful, hip in a quiet, serious way. Completely in tune with the subject of today's telecast. Eden always knew how to set a tone on his program, down to the last detail. You could tell if the show was going to be frivolous and spirited or whether he was going to launch into topics like fen-fen addiction or circumcision or the scourge of hepatitis C among baby-boomers. Loose, open-necked bowling

shirts in hot colors for a show on cosmetic tattoos and dark mono-
chrome ensembles for matters that quickened the national psyche
to outrage.

"Charlotte, welcome. We are indeed honored to have you here
tonight as the spokeswoman for OMEN. Let me preface this by
saying that OMEN—and please jump in here anytime, Charlotte—
is a relatively young organization that is addressing the social and
psychological ramifications of technology, specifically the 'Net.
I find the acronym fascinating. What does it stand for, and how did
your group come up with that?"

"OMEN stands for Overwrought Mothers Enraged about the 'Net.
I guess you could say that it just came to us one day when we were
sitting around talking about how our children were becoming
cyber-dropouts. I experienced that personally with my own little
girls." Tears welled up in Charlotte's eyes. *Girl, you have got it
going on!* Jaqui whispered offstage.

"Oh really!" Eden crossed his legs and drew closer to Charlotte.
"How did this manifest in your own life? And, I might add, no one
on the Chatroom is ever painted into a corner; no one is ever
forced to reveal anything they don't want to reveal. Just remember
that. You don't have to answer any question you don't choose to
answer. I just wanted to clarify that. It's our ethic, the rule we live
by. So tell me more."

"Thank-you, Eden, for the preface. But, I will share parts of my
story because I want mothers out there to understand that we need to
both curb our children from spending too much time on the Web and
to demand responsible content on the 'Net. I started noticing changes

in how my girls were behaving about two months ago. Little things at first. The first thing that I noticed was that they were ignoring me completely, and later that got worse. They started to ignore their schoolwork, the things they used to love doing, like playing with Barbies, and they even stopped communicating with their friends. All they wanted to do was play on the Internet all day. I couldn't even get them to eat meals and go to bed at a decent hour."

"So, for example—and I don't want to put words in your mouth! We don't do that on the Eden Winters' Chatroom. I'm hearing you say that you felt as if you were being edged out of your children's life by the Internet? Is that true? What did that feel like to you?"

"Absolutely. It was pure hell. Oh, I'm sorry, I almost forgot that we're on network television!"

"Heh, don't worry about a little slip like that, Charlotte. Our censors have more important things to do, from what you're saying!"

"Yes, so to go back to my feelings. I felt as if I was losing touch with my own babies. I felt like I was in some dark, scary place where I kept reaching out for them and just couldn't find them any more. They had disappeared into some technological black hole—the sweet little girls I knew and loved—and they turned into people I couldn't relate to anymore no matter how hard I tried."

"So, tell me honestly, Charlotte, and I don't want to plant any thoughts in your mind! Not at all!" Eden sat back in his chair, palms up in front of the camera as if the nose of a gun was wedged in his back. He lowered his chin, and in an earnest tone, asked, "Did your daughters become Internet junkies?"

"Yes! That's the perfect description!" Charlotte's voice cracked, and she burst into a gush of tears. *Oh, this is so perfect,* thought Jaqui. She did that just the way it was rehearsed in the studio a few days ago! *You're a pro, a real pro. Looks like you're not going to need me anymore! Char, you have got a future ahead of you!*

"And, tell me Charlotte, was there something in particular that captured their attention? Any particular site?"

"Yes, there was," she sniffled. "It was Ozzzz.com"

500 individuals in the studio audience gasped in unison. *That is exactly the effect we wanted!* thought Jaqui. *Good move, Eden!*

"Remember, you heard it here first, on Eden Winters' Chatroom! Now, Charlotte, isn't that the site with all of the little games, with Virtual Dorothy, the cyber version of our childhood favorite from Kansas? Pure, sweet, innocent Dorothy, who battles the Wicked Witch?"

"Yes, but it's not as innocent as it used to be, Eden. It's evil. And Virtual Dorothy from Ozzzz.com is evil personified."

"All right, let's get to the bottom of this. It is your contention and the belief of your advocacy group, OMEN, that children are being manipulated in some way by this site, by this Virtual Dorothy character? Let me get this straight. Something happens to kids when they log on to this site. There's some change in behavior that occurs. Is that what you're trying to say?

"Absolutely. Their behavior changes. No question," responded

Charlotte.

"Ladies and gentleman, I want you to hold that thought, and we'll get to your feedback in a few minutes. Just hold that thought. Let me play devil's advocate here for a minute. You know, I checked this out on my own. Now, mind you, I'm coming to this as an adult, and from what you all know of me, I'm hardly a babe in the woods! I personally logged on to the Ozzzz.com site, played the games on a daily basis—dontcha' just love the one with the Wicked Witch of the West—and, here's a secret, I have a garage full of that great stuff they sell on the site—jewelry, puppets, dolls, the works. Yes, I confess. I even own a pair of ruby red slippers. Of course, I only wear them on formal occasions! I'm being flippant, I'll grant you, but what could be so harmful about Ozzzz.com? I love it, and have I turned into some sort of cyber-robot? Well, Charlotte, what do you have to say about that?"

"Eden, with all due respect, can I ask you a question? And I'll stick to your rules—you don't have to answer it."

"Charlotte, you're teasing me. You know, I will answer any question asked of me on air or off air. Shoot."

"Eden, how much money have you spent on Ozzzz.com so far? You know, of course, that every time you open a game, you're getting charged by the minute. And, you know, of course, that if you've joined their so-called community, you give them your credit card number to cover the membership fee. And whatever you do on Ozzzz.com automatically gets billed to your card, and they never ever pop up a confirmation screen when the kids are logged in. So, I go back to my original question, what's your Visa bill been like since you've plugged yourself into the site?"

"Well, I can't recall off the top of my head, but I can check with my personal assistant. Prescott, do you remember what we paid out this month?"

Prescott, a tall immaculately groomed man, who seemed to be attached to Eden's right hip, produced a statement from his shirt pocket and handed it over to Eden with a wink.

"Oh, thank-you so much, Prescott. He is so on the ball! We'd never make it without it him. Come one, everyone, let's give him a hand." Applause rose up and died down as Eden cleared his throat.

"Hmmmm. Well, let's see here. It looks like the total damage for Ozzzz.com spending last month was—Yikes! I'm embarrassed to admit this! $19,890.00. God, Prescott, where were you when I needed you? Maybe I have turned into a droid! Well, moving right along, Charlotte, I think I can see what you're getting at. Am I right when I say that you and your organization, OMEN, Overwrought Mothers Enraged over the 'Net, believe that children—and I guess adults too, so it seems—are somehow per-suaded to spend time and money to line the pockets of a seemingly harmless dotcom company."

"Absolutely! And I have the data to prove it!"

"No doubt! Hey, before we run out of time, let's turn to the studio audience and hear your thoughts. Remember, you are enti-tled to anonymity, so no names, no cities!" Eden rose, remote mike in hand, and cased the audience. He spotted a stocky man in a plaid shirt and shoved the mike in front of him. "Sir, any comments?"

"Yeah, lots. I'm a father of three boys under the age of ten, and I believe that Ozzzz.com is some sort of conspiracy! I'm convinced of that! My kids talk to the computer more than they talk to me! Charlotte, I'm 110% behind you! Hey, can I become an honorary member of OMEN?"

"Thank-you. Over here. Say, you look like a hip young woman. Do you use the 'Net? What are your thoughts on this pressing issue?" A young woman, about eighteen, rose from her seat.

"Um, yeah. I do use the 'Net. It's cool. You can find all kinds of really neat things there, and it's a lot easier than driving all the way to the mall. That's like five blocks away. I would, like, never do that anymore. It's so 20th century. Yeah, I shop on the 'Net all the time. And I looooove Ozzzz.com. I think Dorothy's such an awesome role model. I mean, she's probably like my age or something, and look at her, she's like famous. I would looooove to position myself like that. Besides, I think I'm a lot prettier! "

"Okay, another point of view. Thank you, young lady. By the way, do you have any idea how much you've spent on Ozzzz.com?"

"Oh, nooooo. It's like on my parents' credit card. They don't talk about money and stuff like that in front of me, so I guess it can't be all that much. But come to think of it, they did have to sell one of the SUVs last month. Bummer. I thought that I was going to get that one. Oh, well, I can still shop online."

"Let's move on and hear one more voice. M'am, what about

you? What is your opinion of Charlotte's allegations against
Ozzzz.com?" A middle-aged woman in glasses with a no-nonsense
way about her eagerly took the mike from Eden's hand.

"My name is Eileen Heinz, and I live in the heart of Silicon
Valley. I'm proud to be a member of OMEN, and I am not afraid
of expressing my point-of-view in front of millions. It's time parents, teachers, and concerned citizens sit up and take notice.
Unplug our children from the ravages of this treacherous
technological brainwashing, I say! I am putting out a plea to all of
you to write protest e-mails to Ozzzz.com. Free our children from
this destructive underhanded indoctrination campaign. Ozzzz.com
must go down! Bring back our children!"

The studio audience roared in support. Placards suddenly
appeared, waving messages before the camera. "Heed the Omen!"
"Crash Ozzzz.com." "Dorothy is an e-devil!"

Eden jumped back up onto the stage. "Viewers, it's apparent that
we've hit a nerve here. We'd love to hear your comments, so I
encourage you to join the online Eden Winters' Chatroom to continue
the discussion. Log in at www.Edenchat.com! And don't forget that
you can see a videocast of this week's programming at your leisure.
www.Edenchat.com! So long, folks! We hear you! We hear you!"

Jaqui slipped out from behind the curtain and ran up to Charlotte.
She threw her arms around her neck and gave her a squeeze!

"You've done it, Charlotte. Do you realize that? You've created a
stir! Oh, and Eden, thanks so much for this opportunity! You're an
absolute genius! A genius!" Jaqui grabbed Eden by both shoulders
and imprinted a lipstick mark on each cheek.

"You better watch out! Prescott snarls when he's jealous! But, hey, Jaqui, Charlotte, my pleasure. I think you've got something here. And the world has heard it first on Eden Winters' Chatroom. This is big! Come on, we're running late for lunch. Our publicist is keeping the seats warm over at la Belle Endive. We're going to put on a PR campaign that'll have Sam quaking in his pants in no time."

"What's worse than some person looking into your personal life? A computer."

Paul Saffo, Institute for the Future, Menlo Park, CA, quoted in "Privacy Squeeze" by Sara Solovitch, Science and Spirit Magazine, July-August, 2002.

Chapter 32

Coincidence or Conspiracy?

May 8, 2000

Mothers Voice Concern about Ozzzz.com
Allege Brainwashing of Children

Palo Alto—Once again Ozzzz.com was beset by a wave of negative publicity, as an international organization of mothers publicly leveled allegations that the world's most popular and most profitable on-line children's community is responsible for cultivating anti-social behavior among its young fans. The charges were brought forth yesterday on the globally broadcast talk show, Eden Winters' Chatroom. There is speculation that the recent distributed denial of service attack on Ozzzz.com may be related to the recent uproar.

Charlotte Meyerstone, spokeswoman for OMEN (Overwrought Mothers Enraged about the 'Net), an organization dedicated to protecting children from potentially negative effects of excessive Internet use, claimed that Ozzzz.com contained harmful content, causing social and psychological breakdown among its user base of children under 12. Drawing from personal experience,

Meyerstone suggested that children were being brainwashed by Ozzzz.com, causing them to neglect family, friends and schoolwork and encouraging them to play pay-by-the minute games on the site. She also pointed to examples of excessive credit charges run up by what she termed an "e-commerce mania" in an interview today. Ozzzz.com charges a $29 per month membership fee. Logging on to the many games available on the site results in additional credit card billings. Ozzzz.com also offers a wide array of toys, games, costumes, and memorabilia. Purchases are automatically billed to the credit number entered upon registration for membership without the need for parental confirmation. An OMEN member from the studio audience, Eileen Heinz, put forth a plea to parents to bombard Ozzzz.com with an e-mail protest campaign.

"We've had an amazing response from this programming. It's boosted our ratings 300%," commented Chatroom host Eden Winters. "This far outstrips our program on parental child molestation and schoolyard violence."

This development comes on the heels of a recent distributed denial of service crash of the Ozzzz.com site 3 days ago. The site was inactive for a total of 12 hours, costing the company over $16.9 million in revenue. Shares of the publicly traded company plunged from a high last week of $279 per share to $68.

Sam Thorne, CEO of Ozzzz.com, was unavailable for comment. A company communiqué stated that the site was "solidly back in place with redundant servers and improved security." It further went on to say that "Ozzzz.com carefully screens all content and adheres only to the highest standards for the only highest social good, with the profit motive being a secondary concern." When asked if there was any connection between the recent hacker-instigated crash and protest activities mounted by OMEN, an Ozzzz.com spokesperson responded that the incidents were "most likely unrelated and purely coincidental." The spokesperson explained that attacks of this kind were "fairly typical of the cyberworld, especially when you have a site that attracts such a large international audience like ours."

The matter is pending further investigation by the FBI.

"Private faces in public places are wiser and nicer than public faces in private places."

W.H. Auden, Shorts, collected poems.

Chapter 33

Floodgate

"Greg, there's someone calling for you from Ozzzz.com, believe it or not!"

Mariel handed Greg the portable phone and a tall glass of carrot juice she had just made. He grimaced.

"I thought you said you were getting into carrot juice!" said Mariel, mildly disappointed.

"It's not the rabbit fuel, it's Ozzzz.com. Who is it?"

"She wouldn't tell me her name. Should we put the speaker and recorder on, just in case?"

"You're always thinking ahead. Hey, great juice, really sweet. Okay, put her on."

Mariel squeezed Greg's hand and ruffled his curly brown hair as she flipped on the Polycom conference phone and the record button.

"Hello, this is Greg."

"Greg, it's a voice from the past. Bambi Rose, here, from Ozzzz.com. You might remember me from Prophet Corporation just a few years ago. You and your partner did a human resources survey and assessment for us."

"Oh yeah. Can I put you on hold for a second? I have to grab another line real quick!" Greg pointed to the phone. "Mariel, do you believe this? That bitch has a nerve to call us, after kicking our butts for telling the truth about that hellhole? Oh, this ought to be interesting. I'm going to let her have it."

"Greg, Greg, calm down. Collect yourself. Take a deep breath, look at those ocean waves out the window in front of you. Calm. Soft. Relaxed," coaxed Mariel. She could feel a ballistic episode coming on. Every so often, Greg turned into a defensive, reactive street kid who carried a lifelong grudge against anyone who crossed him in any way. Greg always had a hard time forgiving, forgetting, and staying neutral, even though he was masterful at ingraining those very ideals into the mindset of the toughest business leaders in the industry. Mariel kissed him on the back of his neck and stuck her hand way down his shirt, massaging his chest. "Greg, put the conference phone on. She's waiting."

Greg smiled fondly at Mariel.

"Bambi, I'm back. Sorry to make you wait. What's on your mind?"

"Needless to say, this is not a social call," answered Bambi curtly. "Let's cut to the quick. I would like to offer you $500,000 for the archives of the survey you did at Prophet. Don't tell me you don't have copies. I know we shredded the reports and compacted the tapes, but I also know you two weren't born yesterday. So, I'll put up the cash if you put up the documents and tapes."

"Bambi, before we even start to negotiate, I need to get something off my chest. Believe me, I would never do this with any other client, but I was so absolutely disgusted by—" *Oh, no. He was beginning to rant!* Mariel shook her head and slid down to the floor. Taking both of his feet in her lap, she pulled his socks off and started to gently massage his toes, every so often, slipping her hand up his pant leg and squeezing his hard calf muscle. Greg's face lit up like a child's.

"Excuse me?" said Bambi.

"Oh, I was saying that I was so absolutely disgusted by the loss of those priceless archives. Let me noodle on your offer for a moment. You're saying that the information we assembled back in '94 is worth half a mill to you. What if I were to tell you that as professional psychologists, we have sworn an oath to protect the privacy of our clients and their constituents. In other words, we are duty-bound to protect the privacy of Sam Thorne—CEO of Prophet—and his employees."

Mariel stood up and smiled. She got his blood to pump back up to the brain. *Brilliant move, Greg. Just brilliant!*

"Well, I would have to say it's a crock. I don't care. I don't believe it. And I'll give you $600,000."

"$750,000, and you get the CD-ROM, all neatly archived."

"Okay, it's a deal. Fed Ex me the CD, next day, and I'll send you a check."

"Wire the money to my account this afternoon and as soon as it's in, I'll Fed Ex the CD. Oh, and, by the way, what's your Fed Ex number?"

"You shrinks make me nervous. I'll e-mail it to you."

"Pleasure working with you again, Bambi."

"My admin will take care of the details." Greg clicked off the conference phone and grabbed Mariel around the waist. "I feel like we just won the Lotto. Hey, let's go down to the bank, and I'll treat you to a bowl of chowder at the Sailor's Shanty after."

"Paranoia is synonymous with logic."

Anonymous technical advisor

Chapter 34

Cyber-Sleuthing

Mime-Version: 1.0
Date: Wed, 21 May 15 1:04:09 -0800
To: wocman@ozzzz.com
From: Caitlin Leary <cleary@ozzzz.com>
Subject: Swat team
Status:

Hi Seymour,

I have a directive to assemble a task force to sniff out the hacker attacks. I need the assistance of you and Sampo, so let's meet in my office at 3:30 to strategize.

Caitlin

"Hi, Caitlin, you don't look any the worse for wear today. Here's your mocha, courtesy of the Ozzzzone! You must be pretty steely. I thought for sure that Sam would absolutely roast you alive when I left," Seymour said, parking himself on the edge of Caitlin's desk. Sampo, a small-boned Filipino man, politely drew up a chair and folded his hands in his lap, deferring to his supervisor.

"No, nothing of the kind, actually. All of a sudden, he turned into a total pussycat. It was, well, odd. The whole thing is odd," said Caitlin.

"Well, it sounds like a typical Thorne tactic to me. Let the guillotine drop in the town square and then apologize later. Alas, poor Yorick!"

"Well, let's not get into that right now. We have to roll up our sleeves and get to the bottom of these hacker attacks. Do you think this has got anything to do with all of the e-mail protests we've been receiving from parents and teachers? That seems pretty obvious to me," said Caitlin.

"Yeah, well, of course. The trick is to track down the machines. Right now, as Sampo mentioned yesterday, whoever the general is, he or she is redirecting everything through machines assigned to internal folks, to make it look like an inside job. Pretty clever, I might add. Sounds like something a high-school kid probably couldn't do, especially since we haven't been able to trace the messages to network servers outside of ours. Now, that impresses me!" observed Seymour.

"Okay, so someone's trying to look like they're inexperienced and naïve, when, in fact that person is really quite a pro—a real Wizard, pardon the reference. I'm thinking we could put out an appeal to the hacker community. You know, see if anyone wants to join us in the chase. I'm not too up on that world, Seymour. Where would I go to post a message like that?"

"Now you've got my interest. Being naturally paranoid, I snoop around those underground cyber moleholes quite a bit. I've actually learned a lot that way. Heh, heh, how do you think I've achieved this level of condescension? It's really character building, you know. Anyway, here's the thing. You can't just go busting into a hacker den just like that. 'Oh, hi, fellas, I'm Caitlin from Ozzzz.com, you know, Virtual Dorothy, and I need help!' You'll be laughed off the Internet."

"Geez, Seymour, what do you take me for! I'd feel insulted if I didn't know you better." Caitlin shook her head. Seymour was known to go a little too far at times, but buried somewhere in the complex tangle of wires that looped around his nervous system, she was sure she could detect the beating of a compassionate heart. After all, he jumped in with both feet yesterday, taking up the dragonslayer's sword, in Sam's office.

"Oops, sorry, Sometimes I forget that we have a hierarchy here. It's just that you're so easy to chum around with. All right, back to business. These renegade geeks are a strange lot. I'll have to say, I've never met one in person, but I can just imagine the experience. Frightening. The best thing to do is to win their confidence. Remember, they trust no one. So you have an in, a connection. I've been careful and clever enough to win their respect, especially the notorious jabberjousters. I'll give you the URL and the key code. You'll have to tell them that I sent you, except they don't really know who I am. You have to come up with your own handle too so that you stay anonymous. Are you sure you don't want me to tackle this for you?"

"No, I'll take care of it. I want you and Sampo to keep your eyes on the WOC. Sampo, you take the morning shift, since you have a family, and Seymour, you take the evening shift, since you never get here till 1:30 anyway. I'll be checking in with you both periodically. In the meantime, I'll start cruising the underground sites. Seymour, bookmark as many of those URLs as you can. Meantime, what's your handle for the jabberjousters?"

"Just tell the tribe that 'Slitheytoves' sent ya, and don't tell 'em you work for Ozzzz.com, or you'll get kicked out for sure. Don't forget these guys are anti-social renegades, and they'd love nothing better than to participate in the destruction of Corporate America's infrastructure. It's a paradox, for sure. If they destroy the infrastructure, they'll go down with it, but maybe they have unrealized masochistic cyber death wishes."

"Hey, Seymour, one more question. How in the world do you know all this?" asked Caitlin. She glanced for a moment at Sampo, who never moved during the whole meeting. He smiled sheepishly at her, as if to say, "Don't look at me!"

"Like I said before, I'm gifted with a natural paranoia, so I figure the more I know, the more paranoid I become. But that's a good thing. It's a survival mechanism. I have a theory that the Internet's going to blow up one day. I don't mean literally. All the world's servers won't just crash one day. It has more to do with ripping down the curtain and exposing who's in charge behind the scenes and what their real motivations are. But never mind, we can talk more about that later. Let me do my due diligence, and I'd advise you to keep your head down and check out who's behind you at all times, Caitlin. Glad to be of assistance."

"We had fed the heart on fantasies, the heart's grown brutal from the fare."

William Butler Yeats, "Meditations in Time of Civil War," The Tower.

Chapter 35

Milagros

"Mees Bambi, I have a Fed Ex package for you!" announced Luz into the intercom.

"Luz, that's great, bring it up to my office. I need your help with a few things here. And, hey, could you pour me a nice glass of that La Crema Chardonnay you picked up from Trader Joe's the other day. Fix yourself something, too."

Bambi sat in the middle of the floor of her upstairs home office surrounded by piles of audiotapes, videotapes, and printouts of e-mails and voice transcripts. The Fed Ex package must be Greg and Mariel's CD-ROM archive of the attitudinal assessment that they did for Prophet Corporation fifteen years ago. Bambi reflected fondly on those days, when she and Sam were a hot item, when dotcom companies weren't choking the Valley and the NASDAQ like unwelcome weeds, and when employees pledged a certain amount of loyalty and longevity to companies like Prophet which, with a steady, deliberate pace, infiltrated the infrastructure of corporate America with its indispensable technology. Things were so different, and Sam seemed so different back then. Bambi remembered the wild nights, staying up late at the Fairmont, guzzling vats of champagne after rounds and rounds of cocaine and hot lovemaking. Bambi remembered Sam's zeal, his unbridled energy, which sometimes led him down a path paved with landmines, but he always rebounded from his mistakes with greater clarity and an even greater resolve to go for the brass ring. Now that his success was a fait accompli, Sam had learned to cultivate a detached, calculated persona. And now, he never made mistakes, at least not when it came to business.

Luz walked into the cluttered office carrying a large tray laden with two generous goblets of white wine accompanied by lowfat brie and rounds of sourdough, accented by a white gardenia.

"Oh, and none too soon! Thank-you, Luz, this is a treat! Have a seat on the floor by me. I need for you to help me organize some of this material." Luz placed the tray on the floor and sat down.

"Wait, Luz, what's this weird looking thing wrapped around the flower?" Bambi held up a small silver object in the shape of a heart with an arrow through it.

"Oh, Madam, that is what we call a '*milagro*' in Mexico. It means 'miracle.' It's like a charm to help cure you of whatever is bothering you. I think from what I hear during your parties with the ladies, that you and they suffer so much from that! So I put it there to give you some help."

"Really? So you think that my heart has been broken, Luz?" reflected Bambi. "Well, maybe you're right, maybe you're right. I think your— What did you call it?"

"*Mi-la-gro!*"

"Yes, your *mi-la-gro* is sweet, but, honey, I've got the cure to my affairs of the heart right here in these piles. And, oh, by the way, where's the Fed Ex package?"

Luz handed Bambi the sealed package. Bambi ripped it open to find a CD-ROM in a plastic jewel-case with a note taped to it, folded in half.

We're putting a moratorium on all communication from you or anyone associated with Sam Thorne. You have all you need on the CD. Please do not contact us again.

Some people just don't understand the importance of maintaining positive, ongoing relationships in business, Bambi thought. Oh well, at least, I have the last piece of evidence in my hands now. She munched on a piece of cheese and took a few sips of wine.

"Okay, Luz, here's what I need for you to do. We need to make two copies of everything you see here and put labels on the copies, so that they're identical to the originals. I know there's a lot here, so it may take us a week or so to get through all of this, but it's really important. You can start by photocopying the paperwork and the audiotapes. I'll work on the videos and the CD-ROMs. When we're done with all of this, we have to haul all this to my vault, and the rest of it gets packaged, one for the media, and one for Sam."

"Okay, Mees Bambi, no problema. May I ask you a question?"

"Oh sure, Luz, what is it?

"Why are you making so much work for yourself. Let me tell you something. I know you for a long time, Mees, since you were young and beautiful! And I know you used to be in love with Sam, and now you are very, very angry with him. I am thinking that somehow it is easier to just say some prayers at your altar with the little milagro than to do all of this work to preserve bad memories! All you had to do is ask for help, and the *milagro* will heal your heart! It's true."

"Luz, my darling. You have no idea what is in store for Sam Thorne, and neither does he. Believe me, precious and sweet as your little charm is, my aching heart will be healed a whole lot quicker once I back him into a corner with all of this evidence and nail him for a 49% share of Ozzzz.com."

"I think it is no exaggeration to say we are on the cusp of the further perfection of extreme evil, an evil whose possibility spreads well beyond that which weapons of mass destruction bequeathed to the nation-states, on to a surprising and terrible empowerment of extreme individuals."

Wired Magazine, April 2000, "Why the Future Doesn't Need Us" by Bill Joy

Chapter 36

Shake Down

Mime-Version: 1.0
Date: Fri, 6 May 2000 10:56
To: webmistress@ozzzz.com
From: $am Thorne (sthorne@ozzzz.com)
Subject: Call me
Status:

Bambi,

The neural pathways have been cleared. We're going global.

Call me around 4:30 at the office, and I'll fill you in.

$am

Mo arrived at the office an hour before his shift. He wanted to make sure that Sam would make good on their deal. He'd never known him not to, when it came to money, but Mo learned early on never to have confidence in anyone who commandeered a large fortune and swarms of women and drove a fast car like Sam's Boxster.

From the Ozzzz.com lobby, Mo rang Sam up on his cellphone.

"Hey, Sam, I'm here for my six-month review, just like we talked about. Should I just come right over to your office?"

"Mo, right on, bro'. Yeah, come on over," answered Sam.

Mo waved to the receptionist and walked on through security to Sam's office.

"My man—and you are 'The Man'—have a seat. I hope you don't mind if I partake of a cocktail. Let me get you a soda," Sam said, raising his martini glass.

"Go for it. I'm way beyond getting wigged out by that anymore. It takes a lot to throw me off center."

"Yeah, no kidding. Look, I have the cash for you right here. And some papers for you to sign so that you're eligible for the options. You have no idea what it meant to have you here the other night. You were magnificent!" Sam walked over to his desk, and from the top drawer, pulled out an envelope fat with cash and legal papers.

"For you, citizen Mo!" Sam came up close to Mo and shoved the envelope into his hand. "Do you know that because of you, the entire landscape of human history has been altered, irrevocably?"

"I hope that doesn't mean that I've done somethin' wrong! I guess not, huh, since you're payin' me. All I did was what you told me to do, act natural and dig deep into my soul. Man, that guy pissed me off! I'll tell you what. I sure as hell ain't castin' my vote for him, but I guess you got what you wanted, and so did I. And that's the important thing."

Sam's phone rang. He excused himself and punched the conference button.

"Sam, it's Bambi. You asked me to call you. I'm just about to leave for my biofeedback session, so get to the point."

"Bambi, it was a bloodless coup, thanks to Mo. A perfect piece of psychological engineering. Nothing, but nothing at this stage in the game would have swayed Portell, except bad PR. God bless America and its political process. God bless freedom of speech!"

"Okay, so you've got the Internet wired. That's a major leap. Now we can move forward, unfettered, with the cause. Good move, Sam. Such a smart man, you are! Usually. I've been meaning to talk to you about something that's been on my mind quite a bit lately. It has to do with our sweet innocent girl, Virtual Dorothy, a.k.a. Caitlin Leary. Remember her?"

"Well, yeah, of course. What about her?" Sam turned off the conference phone and picked up the receiver. Mo watched Sam twirl around in his swivel chair with his well-muscled arms crossed over his chest. Mo dropped down his eyelids and slurped on his Coke, pretending to be absorbed in his stock option paperwork. This was a little hard to take. He'd never seen Sam so deflated before. *Boy, that woman, Bambi, is a piece of work. I sure wouldn't want to get on her ugly side.*

"No, no, Bambi, you've got it all wrong. I am not mesmerized by her. Let me explain, for God's sake!" Sam made another circumnavigation. *Boy, she's sure bustin' his chops! I don't know what kind of voodoo that woman does, but it's pretty damn powerful.* Mo noticed that Sam was squeezing the skin between his brows.

"Look, it was part of the experiment. I just wanted to see if the mind-control technology would work on someone like her, a highly intelligent, technically savvy Ph.D. from MIT. Get it?" Mo folded his body into the sofa, hiding behind the papers. He felt his heart throbbing riotously. This was more than he could take. *You harm a hair on that girl's head, Sam, and...* The strains of Bambi's garbled voice on the other end grew louder and louder.

"Okay, okay. Yes, I enjoyed it. I mean, no, I didn't enjoy it. It was for the cause, Bambi. Hear me out!" Sam paused for a moment. "You've got what? Tapes? Videos? Testimony? What are you trying to accomplish here, Bambi Rose?" Sam went silent again. His face turned pallid gray.

"I give up. Send me the stuff, and I'll ask my lawyer to put the paperwork together. 49% holdings. Okay. It's all yours. I don't know how I let you do this to me, Bambi, but I can guarantee you, it won't be for long!" Sam banged the receiver into the phone cradle.

Mo stood up and stuffed the envelope into his shirt.

"Hey, look, Sam, gotta run. I'm starvin' and my shift starts in less than an hour. Thanks, man, thanks a lot. See you around, bud!" Mo lunged for the door and speedwalked across the techno-warehouse floor, through the gilded doors of Ozzzz.com

"'Hush, my dear,' he said; 'don't speak so loud, or you will be overheard—and I should be ruined. I'm supposed to be a Great Wizard.'"

From The Wonderful Wizard of Oz, by Frank Baum, originally published in 1900.

Chapter 37

Disclosure

"Trini, take me away from here. My life is in ruins!" wailed Caitlin into the phone.

She left the boys in the WOC, seeking refuge in her office for a few minutes to regroup and regain her composure. Trini was her anchor, her ballast, her only lifeline to reality. He was consistent and seemingly immune from the contagion of materialism and drivenness that seemed to infect everyone else in the Valley.

"*Preciosa*, I heard about the site. There were a bunch of people in here from Ozzzz.com earlier, and they seemed pretty concerned. How are you? You must be under an amazing amount of stress. I can hear it in your voice."

"Oh, Trini, I wish we could just be transported to another reality right this minute, someplace where life is simple and people are kind. Kansas, Maine, Mexico. Anywhere but here."

"Caitilin, your time will come, and you'll get through this one. Just remember that sometimes we end up in places doing things that may not feed our souls but we come out of the experience with so much wisdom!"

"Oh, Trini, I can't bear it! When's this lesson going to be over?"

"*Dulce amor*, it's never over. If you pay attention, it just gets easier to keep your center in the eye of the storm, though. I'll help you get through this. You know you'll rise above it, and then—wow—how powerful you'll be! And how strong! I can't do it for you, but you know you can come to me whenever you need to."

"Trini, I want to see you tonight. Let me get things under control here, and I'll come by the café around 7:00. I may need to be hooked in with my cell, if you don't mind."

"Caitlin, you do what you have to do. I won't be an obstacle, but I will hold you in my arms all the way."

"Trini…"

"*Qué? Qué?*"

"Oh, never mind. I just want to see you."

Oh my God, I'm almost an hour late! I hope he won't be angry at me!

Though things were under control for the time being at Ozzzz.com, Caitlin felt as if she were walking toward the edge of a cliff in pitch darkness, knowing that at some point, the ground would disappear from beneath her feet. She checked in with the WOC one last time to make sure the site was up, shut down her system, and walked around the corner to the Café Corazón.

Trini was clearing tables from the dinner crowd and seemed unperturbed.

"Trini, I'm an hour late. So sorry! I hope you didn't feel like you had to wait for me!" apologized Caitlin.

Trini came up to her and playfully cupped his hand over her mouth.

"You apologize too much for yourself, Caitlin! I wasn't worried, and my ego's not so fragile! You had business to take care of, that's all. So have a seat at this nice, clean table and talk to me."

Trini placed a cup of coffee in front of her and sat down, taking her left hand in his.

"Trini, I think I've just about reached my limit! I was publicly tarred and feathered by Sam today. It was humiliating and completely groundless. Then, when I was alone with him in his office, he had the nerve to act as if nothing had happened and started his whole seduction routine again. I refuse to be treated disrespectfully—by anyone! I don't care what it costs me! The stock options, the job, Silicon Valley. The whole thing can go to hell in a handbasket! I won't be abused anymore, Trini. I've decided to resign tomorrow."

Trini gave her hand a squeeze.

"Well, the ball's in your court. It sounds like it won't get any better. And you remember the conversation we had a few months ago when Mo brought you over here for dinner—about Sam and his exploits? You see it all now, don't you? I swear I don't know the details and don't choose to know, but I do know that Sam's injured a lot of women in his time."

"Yeah, and he's added another name to his list—the infamous Virtual Dorothy—me—who, by the way, is being deluged with hate mail. Just the other day, I received over 500 e-mails from parents and teachers complaining about how the kids seem to get addicted to the Ozzzz.com site and do nothing but play games and spend money on merchandise. And who do they blame it on—me!"

"Caitlin, that's not the real you! You are right here in front of me at this moment! You can't take it personally! You got sucked into one of Sam's games. You were used! You already know that!"

Caitlin shook her head and was about to speak when the glass door to the café swung open and in walked Mo, heading for their table.

"Mo, speak of the devil. We were just talking about you! What's going on, man, you look upset? Trashed, as a matter of fact," said Trini.

"Trini, I need a Coke, bad. Make it an extra large. You two better hold on to your hats. I have something to tell you that'll take your breath away."

"Sure, man, relax. I'll get you a Coke."

Trini produced a Coke in a flash. Mo took a moment to collect himself. Caitlin had never seen Mo like this before. Usually unruffled and relaxed, Mo was perspiring and panting.

"Mo, you're dripping with sweat! What happened? Don't tell me the site went down again!" said Caitlin.

"I don't know anything about that. But let me tell you, we're not in Kansas anymore. We never were! Caitlin, you've been had. But it's not just you. It's everyone out there, the kids, the parents, the whole world's being conned by Sam Thorne."

"What? What do you mean? What are you trying to say?" asked Caitlin.

"Caitlin, there are things that I found out about you that I know you wouldn't want to tell me yourself. But, we'll let that be. I don't judge, lest I be judged. But I do know what was behind it—what Sam had in mind—and it wasn't just because he was turned on."

"Mo, I'm not sure what you're getting at, but out of respect for the lady here, I don't think we want to hear any of this," intervened Trini.

"You better goddam well hear it. Ozzzz.com is the hotbed of foul intentions and somehow we've gotta stop it! Will you hear me, Caitlin?" begged Mo.

"I'll hear you out, Mo. Trini, it's okay. I've never seen Mo like this, so whatever it is, we owe him an audience."

"All right. As I said before, hold on to your hats. It's something like this—and excuse me if I don't get all the technical jargon. I'm sitting in Sam's office when Bambi Rose calls him. Ain't she a piece of work! And they start in. From what I could hear, it sounded like she was pissin' and moanin' because he's taken a likin' to you and then she started in with all this crazy, threatening talk. Well, you know, Sam, slick and cool as always."

"He sure didn't keep his cool with me today! Sorry, Mo. Go on."

"Hey, no problem. So there he is, in control in his Zen kind of way. He admits it all and then he tells Bambi that you—Caitlin— were part of the experiment. He seduced you to see if the technology would work, that's all. And then he starts braggin' on how the revenues are showin' that the stuff works on the kids and that Bob Portell has bought off on it and they're going to be spreading it all over the Internet!"

"Mo, back up a second. Am I understanding you? He used me to prove a hypothesis? Like I was some kind of lab rat? And he's using the Ozzzz.com site to execute some kind of experiment on the children? This is outrageous! What kind of technology was he talking about? Did he say?"

"Oh yeah, something about neural mapping, and then something else about nano-this and nano-that, that they'd be using in toys and stuff. It sounded like brainwashing to me."

"Whoa, man, no wonder you're upset! This is unbelievable!" Trini jumped out of his seat and started pacing across the room. "This is way beyond just corporate power-tripping! This is like worldwide manipulation. And he had the nerve to try it on my Caitlin!"

Caitlin felt as if the darkness had suddenly lifted. *There's a precipice all right, but now I can see it clearly, so very clearly. And I can't believe how close I've been to slipping into oblivion over the past few months!*

"I get it! I get it! This is absolutely inconceivable. Trini, you are so right! I have been used! I thought I was losing my mind and my will after I was with Sam. He took me into this virtual reality chamber with all of these images, sounds, and smells swirling around. For months, I felt as if someone had put a spell on me, as if I'd been drifting away from myself. And that whole Virtual Dorothy ploy with all of the games, animations and merchandise was nothing but a scam to get these kids enticed into spending more of their parents' money!"

"Caitlin, you never told me any of this! I thought you just kind of fell for the guy's charisma!" said Trini.

"Uh, Mo, not that I'm getting paranoid, but you said you were sitting in Sam's office. Then, you weren't cleaning it. Taking a break, I suppose, or was it something else? Pardon me for being inquisitive, but I guess I've picked up on the Silicon Valley way."

"Aw, Caitlin, I've gotta level with you. I was not cleaning Sam's office. I was picking up my compensation for a special job he asked me to do, okay? I had no idea it was all connected with this kind of thing, and then when I heard about what he was trying to do to you, I really started to boil over! I can understand doing business. I can understand competition. I can understand trying to best someone to get to the top even. But I won't stand for it when someone gets hurt, not physically, not mentally. He's trying to poison everyone's mind so they can do what he tells 'em to do."

"Mo, you've nailed it! It looks like I have my work cut out for me. Trini, I'm not resigning. No, indeed. I will plunge right into my job with all the zeal I had when I first got on that plane to California. This Dorothy's going to crack that code and pull the curtain down around the Wicked Wiz for the entire world to see. Watch me."

"It is always hard to see the bigger impact while you are in the vortex of a change. Failing to understand the consequences of our inventions while we are in the rapture of discovery and innovation seems to be a common fault of scientists and technologists; we have long been driven by the overarching desire to know. That is the nature of science's quest, not stopping to notice that the progress to newer and more powerful technologies can take on a life of its own."

Wired Magazine, April 2000, "Why the Future Doesn't Need Us" by Bill Joy

Chapter 38

Wormwood

<Wormwood>: Hmmmph. EarthShu. So you were sent by SlitheyToves, eh? Okay, that's coolio by me. What's up?

<EarthShu>: *Wormwood, I've heard about your reputation. You're something of a hero among us Grey hats, you know. Wormwood, there's something that's been making me ballistic. Can't stop obsessing over it, in fact. I've been hearing rumors on the QT about corporate machinations on the Internet. This could be monumental.*

<Wormwood>: Yeah, well. ;-) Welcome to the real world. Yawn. Sniff. Scratch. Get to the point. I don't have all day.

<EarthShu>: *Okay, sorry. I know you guys have your work cut out for you. Does Prophet Corporation ring a bell? How about Ozzzz.com?*

<Wormwood>: Ouch! I think I pinched a nerve just processing that through my neural network. Ah yes, the "Thorne" in everyone's side! Looks like the smug SOB is getting his just desserts. I find it highly amusing that the man who would be digital god is being

battered by the world's mothers. It's kind of like a reverse Oedipal complex. Do you suppose he mistreated his own mother?

<EarthShu>: *I can't even go there, but I think you've got it, Wormwood. What you said about your neural network. Are you sure you haven't gotten wind of the rumor?*

<Wormwood>: Whaddya mean? What's Sam Thorne got to do with my nervous system? Other than sparking a pervasive wave of visceral queasiness. Now, if you mentioned the United Coffee Company in the context of my nervous system, I could relate. Immediately, as I savor my fourth cuppa for the night.

<EarthShu>: *What about mind control? Does that conjure anything up for you?*

<Wormwood>: Whoa, there, Earthshu, you're getting awfully familiar fast! I can't answer a question like that. That's personal. Really personal. Do I know you from somewhere? Some chatroom long abandoned weeks ago? You're really pushing those buttons. Watch it. All right, you've got my interest.

<EarthShu>: *So? Can you answer my question?*

<Wormwood>: This is spooky. I think of potato-butts sucking up EMFs from the picture tube—of unfortunate humans turned into e-bots with credit cards on shopping rampage—point, click, rack up the debt!—of dot-commies in pig-hog SUVs buying into the whole cyber-greed reality because they think they're so damn smart. Spooky.

<EarthShu>: *Okay, Wormwood. I think we're tracking. Are you ready? Hold on to your DSL line.*

<Wormwood>: I'm tethered. On the edge of my virtual seat. I've got my popcorn and half gallon of Coke right here by my side. Lights. Camera. Action.

<EarthShu>: *Here's what I heard. An inside source, I'm told. Apparently, Thorne's embedded some sort of mind control technology into the Ozzzz.com site. My guess is that it sends out subliminal messages that are somehow genetically encoded to receptors in the brain and the central nervous system. So when you get zapped, you're not aware of it. You just sort of get injected with this virulent message, if you get my drift, and you carry on like everything is groovy, except that you end up behaving and responding exactly the way Thorne directs you to behave and respond.*

<Wormwood>: You know, not to take any wind out of your sails, Earthshu, I've suspected this ever since the site went live. Too weird. And once they launched the Virtual Dorothy Killer Bimbo, whoa, that really got me going. I can see why everyone's up in arms. I've wanted to crack that one for a while. Been busy, though, with other pursuits, heh, heh.

<EarthShu>: *Oh, yeah, that Dorothy thing is pretty amazing. She's a scary phenomenon. It was bad enough that they came up with the Virtual Newscaster, and now this!*

<Wormwood>: Yeah, and "The Wizard of Oz" was always one of my favorite stories. Now they go and ruin it for a whole generation, with a distorted new millennium e-commerce mind-grab version of

a great story. Now, that's enough to make anyone—especially me—bristly, like a cow with a hemorrhoid.

<EarthShu>: *Oh, it's disgusting! And hey, what do you make of the distributed denial attacks on Ozzzz.com? Do you think it's the work of some bored hacker, or something else, like a protest.*

<Wormwood>: Oh, just a bad "OMEN," pardon the pun. It's obvious.

<EarthShu>: *Yeah, but Thorne's not addressing it in the press. There's been no investigation. He seems to be just blowing it off. You'd think he'd get the Feds involved to protect his business.*

<Wormwood>: Well, ya know what, Earthshu...I think you're on to something. If, like you say—er, excuse me, allege, Thorne's got something going on behind the curtains, of course he won't want the Feds poking around in his infrastructure. I think you've got something here.

<EarthShu>: *Wow! I hadn't thought of that! What a mind, Wormwood. You are so devious!*

<Wormwood>: Yes, er, delightfully devious, if I do say so myself, ahem! But let's not lapse into hero-worship now (you) and ego (me). It looks like I have some work today. Hey, stay connected, okay? Give me 24 hours. Back at ya' later!

Caitlin logged off the chatroom. It was close to 3:00 am, but she wasn't a bit tired. In fact, she hadn't felt this energized since she left Maine. She got up and poured herself another cup of French Roast, a taste she had acquired since her move. There was an immense amount of work to be done. Sitting down at her computer again, she navigated into the central server in the WOC and logged into the directory, protected by several levels of permissions, where the Ozzzz.com graphics and animations resided, before they were prepped for the Web and turned over to her. Methodically, she began investigating the code behind each file, trying to quell her anticipation of her next encounter with Wormwood.

"Biotech firm fixes garbled data

Human DNA appeared in fruitfly sequence

In a scientific mix-up that has gene researchers buzzing, the biotechnology company that deciphered the genetic code of the fruit fly inadvertently included stretches of human genetic material in data it posted on a public Web site.

The genome of any organism—human or fly—is its entire genetic code, contained in long DNA molecules that are made up of four chemical building blocks, identified by the letters A, T, C, and G. There are 3 billion of these chemical letters in the human genome packaged in 23 pairs of chromosomes. In contrast, the fly contains about 180 million letters in just four pairs."

By Paul Jacob and Peter G. Gosselin (Los Angeles Times), San Jose Mercury News, Thursday, April 20, 2000.

Chapter 39

Epiphany

"Trini!" Caitlin heard the soft, measured tempo of the familiar footsteps and flung open the door to her apartment.

"Hi, *Preciosa*!" Trini, boyish in denim cut-offs and a white T-shirt, gently drew Caitlin toward him and embraced her warmly. "I thought I'd swing by. I couldn't sleep all night thinking about you, so I decided to come over…and then I saw that the lights were on in here. I hope I'm not disturbing you. I just wanted to make sure you were okay. You had a fire in your eyes the other night that I've never seen before."

"Trini, you're looking at a woman on a mission. I think I've got the man—at least I think he's the man for the job," Caitlin said, pacing back and forth across her livingroom.

"You mean to help you crack the mind-control technology? That's incredible news, Caitlin! Who is he?" Trini settled into the couch, scrunching a throw pillow behind his back.

"Oh, well, actually I don't know who he is. I just know that he calls himself 'Wormwood,' and he despises Sam Thorne!"

"Hey, that's great. So who doesn't…so what is this Wormwood dude going to do for you? I hope he won't make me jealous!"

"No way, Trini! He's probably some undernourished guy with crossed eyes and terminal psoriasis. Don't give it a thought. Apparently, though, from all the talk in the hacker chatrooms, he's the arch black hat."

"Oh, like in a Western. There are the guys in the white hats and the guys in the black hats. So does that make him a good guy or a bad guy?"

"Well, it depends on what side of the fence you're on. Right now, to us, he's a good guy, and to Thorne, he's a bad guy. Even though Wormwood calls himself a black hat."

"Okay, I think I get it. If you say so. You know what you're doing. It's all Greek to me. Or should I say, it's all 'geek' to me?"

"Trini! I know you think I'm getting a little squirrelly, but I've been doing a little digging around myself. I was able to pull the raw graphic files from the Ozzzz.com server and tear through the source code. I know this won't make much sense to you, but I found some really bizarre strings of code in there. None of it makes much sense to me, but I'm sure it must mean something. When you see a pattern, a repetition, then there's a meaning behind it."

"Sure, like a secret language that maybe only a few people know, or maybe we all know it on some level, but can't verbalize it."

"What do you mean? Stay with that thread, Trini. Just keep talking."

"I was just thinking that it reminds me of my grandfather. He was a doctor, but not like the doctors here at Stanford. People would come to him with illnesses, sometimes physical and sometimes emotional, and he would just get quiet and look deeply into their eyes and start talking about the things he knew. He'd tell them what remedies to take, what signs to watch for, and he never even cracked open a book. He just knew, like he had Xray vision and could read their cells and all of the genetic coding. And, believe it or not, just about everybody got better!"

"Yeah! Okay, so something we know but we don't know how to verbalize. Trini, there's something to that. I keep seeing strings of letters inserted into the source code that don't make any sense. But like you said, on some level, I know what they mean. The letters A, T, C, and G keep showing up in different combinations and strings, hundreds of them." Caitlin flopped onto the couch, leaning into Trini. "Trini, you know what? I can't think anymore."

"Caitlin, I can tell. Relax and forget about all of it for a little while. Here, put your head in my lap." Trini reached for a pillow and slipped it under Caitlin's head.

Caitlin savored the healing touch of Trini's warm, reassuring hand stroking her hair. She felt her eyelids getting heavy and her body collapsing into the welcoming surrender of deep rest. Floating in a zone somewhere between consciousness and the deepest slumber, she became aware of a fond and familiar presence. A male voice with the melodic lilt of an Irish brogue whispered words that she was too exhausted to comprehend, so her mind filed them away for later. Swirling around her visual field she fixated on a ceiling dome with an inscription in a mysterious code, an esoteric language of ancient scientists that held "the key to life itself." Each of the symbols presented themselves to her with astounding clarity, imprinting themselves on her consciousness, indelibly. Caitlin quieted herself for a moment and closed her eyes, hearing only the cadences of her own slow, rhythmic breathing and the Gaelic voice. Suddenly, it became clear. The symbols swirled around her in a blur like a pin-wheel and stopped, casting her for a moment in Bambi Rose's livingroom. Caitlin recalled her strange fascination with the inde-cipherable inscription painted around the rim of the domed ceiling. There was some connection, obviously, but she was at a loss at this moment to decipher the cryptic messages that came surging into her consciousness during this half-dream state.

"Caitlin, you have the key. It's in your hands...the key to life itself. Remember that, girlie, you alone have the key to life itself..."

"Company decodes human DNA string

Washington (AP)—A private company mapping the human genetic blueprint said yesterday that is has completed a major step—decoding all of the DNA pieces that make up the genetic pattern of a single human being.

The milestone puts the company, Celera Genomics of Rockville, MD, far ahead of an international government effort to map the human genome using a different method.

'We've now completed the gene sequence plan of one human being,' said Craig Venter, chief scientist for the company. He said that the human being was an unidentified male, adding, 'By the end of the week, we will have finished the gene sequence for a female.'

...In testimony before Congress, Venter said yesterday that this company will make the entire genome available on the Internet, but will provide special services for analyzing the massive amounts of data to drug companies and to universities for a subscription price—in the millions for drug companies and in the thousands for universities."

Palo Alto Daily News, Friday, April 7, 2000.

Chapter 40

Keeper of the Key

"Grampa Leary!" Caitlin awakened from sleep, finding herself lying next to Trini. She noticed that she was wearing her favorite pajamas with red chili peppers dancing on a white background.

"Caitlin, what is it?" Trini grabbed Caitlin's hand.

"I had this dream again about Grampa Leary. He told me I had the key to life itself…we were talking about that last night, remember? Hey, how long have I been sleeping? What time is it? Boy, I need to get hacking and cracking!"

"It's 8 in the morning, Caitlin. You needed the sleep, so I tucked you in. You're safe, I promise."

Caitlin looked down at the pajamas that enveloped her slim frame and giggled.

"These are my favorite pj's. How did you know? I must really have been in a fog. I don't even remember putting these on or walking over here to the bedroom."

"You did pretty well, walking around in your sleep, as if you had the layout of your apartment memorized. You managed not to bump into anything, either. And, let me tell you, you were talking a blue streak."

"I was?" she asked incredulously. No one had ever accused her of talking or walking in her sleep. She laughed. "Maybe this was some kind of new behavior induced by Sam's mind control programs!"

"Oh, yeah! You kept talking about having the key to life itself. And then, you kept saying something about the dome, something about reading the writing on the wall. You said that it was the key to life itself."

Caitlin grasped her head. "Trini, let's get some coffee going. I think some of this is coming back to me. What else did I say?" she asked, flinging the covers off and padding off to the kitchen. Trini bounded out the bed and followed her, intercepting her in front of the coffeemaker.

"Here, let me. I brought some of my special brew from the café. It's a blend I created called *Corazón Caliente*. Anyway, back to your question. You kept talking about strings of code, not computer code, but about DNA code," Trini continued as he deftly prepared two mugs of aromatic coffee topped off with milk that he had warmed up in a saucepan.

"DNA? I'm a software weenie! I don't know anything about genetics! Where did that come from. This is too bizarre! I need to get online and find Wormwood again. I need to send him all of the code I found with the repetitive strings, remember, the letters A, T,

C, and G that I discovered in zillions of different combinations. I have this feeling he knows something I don't."

"But Caitlin, do you think he'll be awake at this hour?"

"You've got a point, but you know what, I can just picture this character with the computer wired to his body, sending off signals to wake him when he gets pinged with e-mail."

"You mean people live like that?"

"Well, let's put it this way, it's not the norm, but in the realm of possibility, and probability, I would guess—from what I saw at school—with these wild-eyed hackers."

"Okay, *Preciosa* , I'll leave you alone. Listen, I need to get ready and help out at the café. Call me if anything big breaks, okay?"

"I promise, Trini, that you'll be the first and only one to know, at least until I have my story together. And, Trini…"

"Yeah, Caitlin?"

"Thanks for being so good to me," Caitlin threw her arms around Trini and tucked her head into the hollow of his neck. Trini engulfed her in his arms, and taking her face in his broad hands, kissed her on the lips.

"Caitlin, I just can't help myself around you, that's all there is to it. You do have the key to life itself, right here." Trini gently pressed his palm against Caitlin's heart. "Call me, okay? I have a very good feeling about all of this, Caitlin. I really do."

Trini withdrew and departed like a whispered promise. *He's not just alluding to my mission. I need to get to the bottom of this right now—for me, for Trini, for the sake of society. Wormwood, you can't let me down!*

Caitlin, feeling full of resolve, logged on to the hacker's chatroom. She announced her presence, calling out for Wormwood.

–

<Wormwood>: So, it's you again. Earthshu. Yup. Yup. Yup. I do believe we are close to striking gold, citizen Earthshu. You show me yours, and I'll show you mine.

Caitlin copied and pasted in examples of the strings of code she had isolated with various combinations of the letters A, T, C, and G.

<EarthShu>: *So, Wormwood, what do you make of these repetitive strings, some of them with variable combinations but all using the same building blocks?*

<Wormwood>: Like you said last night—we're definitely tracking. I noticed that too. I haven't quite completed my count yet, but there were something like 25,783 references of this type on the Ozzzz.com site. I counted the different groupings—it boils down to about 19, give or take. This slimy stuff is sprouting up everywhere—it's sitting behind the e-commerce engine, it's embedded in the animations and games, in the video clips, the

graphics, and even the HTML. It's like a fungus that has crept into every nook and cranny of the Ozzzz.com site.

<EarthShu>: *Yeah, I noticed that too. What's behind, though. What does it all mean? Is it just some sort of strange encryption code, or something else?*

<Wormwood>: Earthshu, are you sitting down this time? Are you? I sure hope so because what I have to tell you is absolutely mind-blowing stuff.

<EarthShu>: *Wormwood, give it to me!*

<Wormwood>: Okay. Leave it to Wormwood and friends and relations. Let's just say that, lucky for you and the world at large, I am virtually the most connected person out in the cyber-universe. Wormwood here has tapped an incredible well of hidden resources, from a medieval linguistic specialist to a giant in the field of genetic engineering, not to mention my small, but well-trained army of kamikaze hackers. There are several things operating here at once. I won't bore you with the details right now—e-mail to follow for sure—in exchange for a favor, of course, but we'll get to that in a minute.

<EarthShu>: *Wormwood, you slay me! I can't stand the suspense. And as for the favor, let me just say that anything is possible.*

<Wormwood>: Okay. Here's the broad sweep. You know those letters you kept finding, A, T, C, and G? Those are the basic elements of the human genome. And some of the particular combinations we found are codes that trigger very specific responses in the

human brain, in particular the part of the brain called the limbic system. They call it the reptilian brain because it's the most primitive portion of the human brain. That's where emotional patterns are stored and processed and then triggered automatically, so that most humanoids—myself excluded, heh, heh—I'm beyond all that—aren't conscious of what or why a particular emotional response is triggered. They just feel it, and it takes over their logical functioning. So what my comrades and I are seeing in operation on Sam Thorne's "children's community" is nothing short of an insidious attempt to manipulate young minds into clicking for dollars, getting them completely hooked on Ozzzz.com to buy more stuff and spend more time there, and eventually become completely transformed into Ozzzz-bots.

<EarthShu>: *Are you serious? I'm speechless. I know guys like Thorne are greedy bastards, but you suppose there's more to it than that?*

<Wormwood>: Well, Earthshu, I'm been around the cyber block for a while, and all I can say is that it's never been done before. That should tell you something.

<EarthShu>: *That it's never been done before? Of course, all scientific endeavors begin with the formulation of a hypothesis followed by a series of well-formulated experiments. So, can we conclude that Ozzzz.com is a mind-control experiment, then, above and beyond the greed factor?*

<Wormwood>: Yup. There seems be a general consensus around here that your conclusion rings true.

<EarthShu>: *And to what end, then, do you think?*

<Wormwood>: Earthshu, Earthshu. Earth to Earthshu. Have you been lost in Birkenstock bliss all your life? Haven't you heard of the WTO? Or the International Monetary Fund? The World Bank?

<EarthShu>: *Well, yes! Of course! Go on.*

<Wormwood>: Don't you see it? It's the global corporate oligarchy at work. We're all wired. It's the religion of the 21st century—the information age has spawned worldwide homogenization. We don't think for ourselves anymore. We think, feel, consume, what the corporations feed us, and what better vehicle for high-level, high-speed propaganda dissemination than the World Wide Warp! Don't you see? Individuals like Thorne are attempting to create a generation of compliant bots who thoughtlessly drone the mainstream mantras of unconscious consumption and complacency. And its done effortlessly through the dynamic technological duo of genetic engineering and the 'Net. Just wire yourself up and no worries, you'll be uploaded with your behavioral and emotional instruction set. You don't even have to think about it or ask for it. It's free. Free mind-altering information for your mind-altering pleasure. And it doesn't matter if you're from Botswana or Peru or Romania. This stuff cuts across linguistic boundaries and hits you right on your neural synapses. Not to mention the fact that you're never alone on the 'Net. Someone's always watching. We're all basically sitting ducks if this code gets disseminated throughout the Internet. Had enough?

<EarthShu>: *Yes…and no. Wormwood, this is enough to make me want to unplug forever and live with the aborigines. Though, sigh, they probably have T1 lines now in the Outback. But hey, there's one more thing I found in the Ozzzz.com code. Every 100,000 lines*

*or so, I found these weird symbols—I know I've seen them before.
I just can't remember where. Here's a sample…*

Caitlin cut and pasted a few samples of code containing arcane-looking symbols that might have come from a medieval hand-lettered manuscript or the Dead Sea Scrolls or something buried in the Ark of the Covenant. Her body shivered as she sent Wormwood the unintelligible symbols. On some level, she felt like she had seen or known the odd curlicues and strokes of these characters before.

<Wormwood>: Ah, very interesting indeed. I know exactly what this is. The language of medieval alchemists—the sorcerer scientists
of olde tymes who claimed that they held the key to life itself.
These are their symbols, their language. They transcribed all of their secret processes, like using human blood as the catalyst for the creation of gold, into this encrypted language. This was the key code—the key to life itself—not so different, I might add from the A, T, C, G combination.

<EarthShu>: *The key to life itself? Wormwood, veritable bottomless well of knowledge that you are—I don't get it? Is this some kind of joke? I don't mean the genetic coding. I mean this medieval script. What's up with that? What do you mean by the "key to life itself."*

<Wormwood>: Oh that! It's just that the alchemists had this notion—realized, by the way, in today's genetic cloning experiments—that they could actually create or alter life in their laboratories through a combination of crude chemistry and magic, black magic. So, how does all of this relate to the mind-control code? I'd have to do more research, but my guess is that whoever

came up with this reprehensible mind mold was into the occult. It could just be their signature. A lot of coders like to sign their work, inserting off-key jokes or their girlfriend's names, that kind of thing.

Say, Earthshu, I need to go in a few…have a standing engagement at the Jabberwocky every Friday. But before I sign off, I want to get back to that special favor I alluded to earlier.

<EarthShu>: *Yeah, okay, I'm all ears.*

<Wormwood>: We—you and I—are in possession of some pretty amazing information. Do you realize, Earthshu, that we could be making history? Do you? Well, I don't want to be the one to do it. I'll do the grunt work. I'll get in there up to my elbows, dissect the code, do the reverse engineering, and feed you all of the information you want. I would like nothing better than to see Thorne and his ilk get exposed and subsequently crushed. But I want no credit, no publicity. You and your alliances can go for the jugular. I just want to sit and enjoy the drama. Okay? Is that a deal? Hacker's honor?

<EarthShu>: *Hacker's honor. My lips are zipped. And, Wormwood… you just made my day. Is it all right if I shuffle and scrape before we part?*

<Wormwood>: Like I said last night. No hero worship allowed. We're all in it for the sport of it! Later, Earthshu!

Caitlin logged off the chatroom and checked her e-mail. He delivered on his promise! She scrolled through hundreds and thousands of lines of Wormwood's thoroughly annotated code. She backed up the file and hit the print command.

While the laser printer churned out reams and reams of code, Caitlin grabbed her cell phone to ring up Trini.

"Trini! I've got the key! Pack your bags! Come over whenever you close up the café. And I'll book a flight for Sunday. This Virtual Dorothy's going home where she belongs!"

"Investigators are trying to determine if associates of suspected terrorism mastermind Osama bin Laden issued secret orders on-line using a modern-day version of an ancient communication method called steganography.

Steganography means 'covered writing,' such as invisible ink. In the computer world, the technique involves hiding a message inside a routine picture, a music file or video that is placed on Web sites or sent through e-mails."

Knight-Ridder Newspapers, October 11, 2001

Chapter 41

Media Blitz

May 28, 2000

Mysterious Hacker Cracks Ozzzz.com.
Investigations Under Way to Determine if Website
Is a Front for Brainwashing Experiment

San Francisco, CA— Ozzzz.com, the popular children's online community, brainchild of Silicon Valley techno-mogul Sam Thorne, is under investigation for possible consumer fraud, invasion of privacy, and distribution of questionable content to minors. News bureaus across the nation received anonymous envelopes containing a document analyzing the code behind the site. The unidentified author of the document alleges that Ozzzz.com is a front for mind control experiments designed to influence the behavior and thoughts of the site's visitors. According to the document, the code, buried behind the whimsical animations, interactive games and online store, was found to convey messages encouraging children to charge more goods to their parents' credit cards, spend more time on the pay-per-play online games and embrace Ozzzz.com as the ultimate source of all truth.

The news bureaus interviewed all received identical packages. Thick brown manila envelopes stuffed with pages of code were dropped at the doorstep of major Bay Area news bureaus. Technology editors and business editors from news bureaus in other parts of the country received the pages via U.S. mail, postmarked from airports in various parts of the country. No one received the tip via e-mail. No one received a single telephone call. There was no electronic trail to follow.

Justin Donleavy, Senior Online Technology Editor at CNN, said that he is "mystified by the whole affair, but impressed with the level of technical knowledge and expertise displayed in the documentation." He added that plans are underway to determine the validity of the "mystery hacker's" findings. CNN, along with ZDNet, The Wall Street Journal, Knight-Ridder Publications and major network news channels have joined forces to present the documents for further investigation by a team of experts collected from the country's top scientific and technical institutions, including MIT, UC Berkeley, Sun Microsystems, Geron and others. The Federal Trade Commission reported that it would step in as soon as definitive results are in to determine whether Ozzzz.com has violated the privacy of its subscribers. A spokesperson for the FBI said that the agency would work hand-in-hand with the FTC to investigate the implications of the charges outlined in the document. Currently, the FBI has no leads on the identity of the document's author.

At Ozzzz.com, it is business as usual. The site itself has remained undisturbed for over a month, since it was shut down by hacker attacks in May. Only a few weeks ago, Ozzzz.com was accused on the nationally televised Eden Winters' Chatroom of encouraging anti-social behavior among its users, most of whom are under the age of 12. Members of OMEN, or Overwrought Mothers Enraged about the 'Net, alleged that the site was responsible for unhealthy behaviors among children, ranging from obsessive consumerism and brand identification with Ozzzz.com to apathy with regard to school-work and family. It has not yet been determined whether OMEN's public outcries are connected to the recent distributed denial of service or the printed document now in the hands of the media.

CEO Sam Thorne of Ozzzz.com could not be reached for comment. However, Bambi Rose, the company's Vice-president of Public Affairs said, "We at Ozzzz.com are committed to continu-ing to
offer only the most wholesome entertainment and educational content to our subscribers. We have always adhered to the strictest standards when it comes to issues of personal privacy and ethical Web business practices."

Ozzzz.com shares, traded on the NASDAQ exchange closed at an all time low of $3 per share.

"Anything that can go wrong, will."

Murphy's Law

Chapter 42

Just Desserts

This evening's ensemble, Bambi noted, as she carved out a hunk of triple cream New York cheesecake with her silver fork, was the epitome of unadorned dotcom chic—crisply-pressed Ralph Lauren khakis and a cadet-blue button-down shirt. Eden Winters' only concession to glitz tonight was a thick solid-gold Rolex. Bambi propelled the cheesecake into her mouth and chased it with a spoon-ful of Lappert's Hawaiian coconut-mango ice cream as she watched her empire being publicly condemned by network television.

Leaning forward earnestly to address the viewing audience, Eden spoke with a solemn timber in his voice.

"Tonight, all of America is witnessing an unveiling…the unveiling of corporate America. Tonight, you and I are privileged to participate in a significant historical moment, a moment fraught with meaning for all of us. Ladies and gentlemen, tonight we will be experiencing a moment of truth with wide-ranging implications for our relationship with technology going into the new millennium. On this stage, we have as our extra special guest, the mystery hactivist who uncovered the horrific secrets buried behind the seemingly innocent façade of

Ozzzz.com, the Website favored by millions of children worldwide."

Bambi leaned over and grabbed at the box of Godiva buttercremes. She stuffed one into each cheek and chewed slowly as tears streamed down her flushed cheeks. My Chardonnay! Where's my Chardonnaaaay! Eden Winters introduced the mystery hactivist, a black silhouette wearing what looked like a fedora, sitting behind a black scrim. Bambi stood up in the midst of a ravaged feast of every conceivable gourmet dessert available and several empty wine bottles and shouted "Luz, get over here, this minute!"

"Sir, I know that your identity is a sensitive matter, so trust me, we will not go there. No, not even for a moment! But tell me, what drove you to dissect the source code behind the Ozzzz.com Website to begin with?" asked Eden.

With a gravelly, low voice that sounded like someone sloshing marbles in his mouth, the hacker spoke:

"To undermine Sam Thorne's diabolical distortion of the greatest children's story in America! To nuke Sam and his corporate oligarchy."

"Oh, you cowardly little menace to capitalism, you screwed it all up!" said Bambi aloud to the ultra-widescreen, surround-sound enhanced television. "Sam, yes! Corporate oligarchy, no! You botched the whole thing you intellectual toad! I had my own plan to bring Sam down, and you ruined it for me! You ruined it all. I don't need another tax loss write-off, goddam you!"

Bambi bent down and hammer-locked an empty wine bottle by its long, thin neck. She heaved it toward the tube, ready to strike when Luz walked in, rolling a silver teacart.

"Mees Bambi—that's very dangerous! I think you should put the bottle down and turn off the show. I made some nice cappuccinos for us. It will be delicious with all of your lovely desserts." Luz pushed the cart out of the way and gently wrested the bottle from Bambi's hand, clicked off the power button on the remote control and led her mistress by the hand to the sofa.

She's spoiling it for me too! I don't want any goddam Italian rotgut coffee. I want my Chardonnay! Damn Luz, fifteen years and she still hasn't learned to listen to me. I should put her on probation again!

Luz quietly and calmly arranged two cups of cappuccino, linen napkins, and tiny silver spoons on the carved crystal coffee table while Bambi fumed with her arms crossed.

"Okay, now that's better. If you please, Mees Bambi, have a sip, and I will join you. There is something I need to talk to you about."

"Well, Luz, there's something I need to talk you about. I am so tired of having to repeat everything. You never listen to me, Luz. You never did. Nobody ever did, or ever does! Sam sure never did!"

"Mees Bambi, calm down. Perhaps you are right. I didn't listen enough for fifteen years. Well, now I decided to listen. To myself," said Luz, delicately sipping her cappuccino.

"So get to the point. You know I hate it when people aren't direct with me, Luz. What are you trying to say?"

"Mees Bambi, I have packed my bags. I am leaving for Guatemala to go home for good. My family, they have been missing me so much, and I miss them too! My mother and my brothers and sisters. Oh sure, they like that I am sending them American money every month, but they love me even more. For many years, now, they have been begging me to come back, and so, I have decided to go."

"But Luz, you can't just walk out like that! I won't allow it! Why is everyone walking out on me! Luz, you can't leave me alone, not now!" Bambi clutched Luz's shoulder. Startled, Luz drew herself back and watched her cappuccino cup tumble down, dribbling brown espresso onto the white carpeting.

"Oh, Mees Bambi. I am so clumsy! Let me clean this up!"

"No!" Bambi shouted. "Stop that! You can't just up and leave like that. Luz, Luz, what will become of me here in this God-forsaken valley, all alone, without a purpose, without a friend! WITHOUT ANY MONEY!"

"I am so sorry for you, Mees Bambi, but my family has been crying for me. It is time for me to go home. I have something I want to give you, though. Remember those '*milagros*' we were taking about a little while ago. I have one for you...that little silver broken heart. I will pray to the Virgin for your healing."

Luz presented Bambi with a tiny white box decorated with an oversized ribbon and a sprig of lilac. Bambi clutched the gift to her breast and bawled while Luz silently slipped through the door and down to the foyer where a taxi awaited her.

"The prevailing attitude among the digerati seems to be that the battle is already over. Scott McNealy, the CEO of Sun Microsystems, has been quoted as saying, 'You already have zero privacy. Get over it.'

And legislation to curb online spying has gone nowhere. Sen. Robert Torricelli's recent bill requiring Web sites to ask users' permission before gathering or selling personal information was beaten back by the high-tech powers who whined that it would stifle business on the Internet."

"Clinic Open for Consumer Caught in the Net"
by Reynolds Holding, Holding Court

Chapter 43

Behind the Curtains

June 3, 2000

Wizard of Ozzzz.com Exposed!
Feds Slam Sam Thorne for Internet Mind Control Experiment

San Jose, CA—Silicon Valley cyberwizard Sam Thorne, CEO of Ozzzz.com and founder of Prophet Corporation, was indicted today by federal prosecutors on multiple counts for consumer fraud, invasion of privacy, distribution of questionable content to minors, and conspiracy charges. This comes on the heels of recent evidence uncovered by an unidentified hacker that the Ozzzz.com online children's community was in reality a front for a mind-control experiment designed to influence children to march in lock-step to the dictates of Ozzzz.com. Mysterious documents which analyzed the source code behind the Ozzzz.com site were sent anonymously to the media and revealed that the code embedded in the site's games, animations, e-commerce shopping arcade, and chatrooms were spiked with subliminal messages. The courts have issued an injunction to shut down the site indefinitely.

The documents, which were thoroughly analyzed by the nation's top technologists and scientists, prove that Thorne's company was influencing the behavior and spending patterns of its young visitors, typically between the ages of 6 to 12. Some of the messages included: "Stop listening to anyone else. Ozzzz.com is the only voice of truth." "Ozzzz.com products and games are your only source of joy." "Be cool. Buy from Ozzzz.com." "Obey Ozzzz.com, not your parents or teachers."

These messages were not apparent to the average Internet surfer. The team of experts engaged by the media to investigate the "mystery hackers" findings discovered that the messages interspersed in the source code were actually fragments of the human genome, which were designed to trigger certain responses in the brain. The code was arranged in certain patterns that transcended language, culture, and socialization, so that an immediate emotional response could be elicited without the awareness of the children who regularly used the site.

According to neurologists and child psychologists, the impressionable nature of children's brains made them particularly vulnerable to this technology. It appears that the effects could range from obsessive-compulsive behaviors to unquestioning obedience to the commands issued through the subliminal messages. World-renowned child psychologist Otto Kinderhopf suggests that "these techniques are based on an extremely sophisticated understanding and implementation of primitive imprinting." Kinderhopf added, "Whoever developed this code had an excellent understanding of the human learning experience. When we are still very young, we are like thirsty sponges, taking in the stimuli offered up to us by our surroundings very rapidly and unquestioningly. It is a basic survival mechanism. As children, we absorb information quickly, and we have not yet completely developed the power of discernment to know what is valid information and what is not."

The FBI has subpoenaed all source code, documents, and recorded material from the Ozzzz.com facility in Palo Alto, California. In addition to computer records, agents also seized crates full of audio and videotapes from Thorne's office, where he had a highly sophisticated surveillance system that could monitor the entire corporate office. The FBI plans to make a complete study of these tapes to determine the intent behind Thorne's operation.

Thorne has been charged with violating the Children's Online Privacy Protection Act, which requires Websites to obtain verifiable parental consent "before collecting, using or disclosing personal information from a child younger than 13." Additionally, he is facing criminal charges for contributing to the delinquency of minors. An organization known as OMEN (Overwrought Mothers Enraged about the 'Net) has accused Ozzzz.com of "turning our precious children into greedy, disrespectful, larcenous liars and thieves," according to spokeswoman Charlotte Meyerstone.

The Justice Department is also looking into possible abrogation of First Amendment rights by intentionally commandeering the will, behavior, and thoughts of children who participated in his virtual community, creating barriers to the free flow of ideas, opinions, and independent choice. Thorne is also being investigated for possible conspiracy charges, based on the political implications of the use of his technology.

Thorne was unavailable for comment.

"And, oh Aunt Em! I'm so glad to be at home again!"

From The Wonderful Wizard of Oz, by Frank Baum, originally published in 1900.

Chapter 44

No Place Like Home

In Rockington, the ocean waters were calm in the summer. No crashing dramatic displays of surf, just white ribbons of foam rolling in a serene rhythm over the sun-bleached shore.

Caitlin felt all cares and concerns melting from her body as she stood, toes dug into the cool, moist sand, where land and water met, content to simply be. She put her hand in the back pocket of her jeans and drew out a small metal object that she tucked into Trini's hand. Wordlessly, Trini accepted and turned to Caitlin, awaiting further instructions.

"We're only a few hundred feet from it," she said. "C'mon, I'll race you!" Caitlin tore away, kicking up clouds of white sand, as Trini followed.

Trini caught up with Caitlin and gathered her up in his arms from behind, reaching out to touch the blue wooden door of the tiny clapboard shanty. His fingers traced an invisible outline around the curves of a carved red wooden heart that graced the door.

"This is my *corazón*! You never told me about this!" he laughed.

"Trini, you know what? I never really paid much attention to it till now! Sometimes, you need other people to point out the obvious! Well, Trini, are you just going to stand there staring, or are you going to use 'the key to life itself'?"

Trini took the silver key that Caitlin had slipped into his hand and inserted it into the lock. With a quick twist and a gentle push, the door flew open, releasing a flood of memories in Caitlin's mind. *This was home, and there really, really, was no place like it.*

"Caitlin, this is perfect! I couldn't have done better in my dreams! What a view, and the ambience is indescribable. We could have dried ancho chili wreaths over on this ceiling beam!" noted Trini.

"Yes, and nets full of seashells and starfish in front of the windows!" said Caitlin.

"Oh, and we'll cover this wall with hand-painted Mexican pottery and coconut masks!"said Trini.

"Yeah, and on every table, we'll have antique sailor's lanterns and make hand-lettered menus on old maps!"

"*Absolutamente*, and we'll have the servers dress up all in white with colorful hand-woven vests!"

"And for the dinner crowd, we can have them sing old Celtic love ballads and Irish sea chanteys!" added Caitlin

"And I'll do all the cooking…"

"And I'll spread the word…but no Website, I promise!"

Caitlin and Trini both paused for a moment, looked at one another, and burst out in a gale of simultaneous laughter. They stepped toward one another slowly as if performing the steps of a sacred dance.

"Caitlin, *mi Preciosa, tu eres mi corazón*," said Trini, brushing a few windswept locks off her forehead.

"And Trini, you're my one and true laddie!" responded Caitlin, stroking his tawny cheek, moistened by a solitary tear.

For the first time in her life, Caitlin felt the fullness of love erupting from her heart and arcing like water spraying from a fountain out into the space around where she and Trini stood.

There was nothing more to want and nothing more to accomplish.

CPSIA information can be obtained
at www.ICGtesting.com
Printed in the USA
FSHW010136230721
83400FS